SIPHONOPHORE

Jaimie Batchan grew up in Hook Norton, a village on the edge of the Cotswolds famous for its beer. He has lived in various places including Reading, Oxford, Lancaster and Ljubljana, Slovenia, where he worked as an English teacher, copy-editor, proof-reader and football journalist. He currently lives in East London with his partner and daughter and co-produces the literature podcast *Unsound Methods*.

Siphonophore

JAIMIE BATCHAN

Valley Press

First published in 2021 by Valley Press
Woodend, The Crescent, Scarborough, YO11 2PW
www.valleypressuk.com

ISBN 978-1-912436-54-5
Cat. no. VP0175

Cover design by Martina Klančišar and Peter Barnfather.
Cover photograph by Matty Smith.
Map illustration by Martina Klančišar.
Text design by Peter Barnfather.
Edited by Jamie Firby.

Printed and bound in Great Britain by
Imprint Digital, Upton Pyne, Exeter.

Acknowledgements

Martina and Iskra, Mum, Dad and Matt. The Hooky Boys and my Sugar Spun Sisters. Those who showed a stranger some love and helped me find the way in Ljubljana in '07 & '08. Those who tolerated my experiments in Lancaster in '09 & '10. The readers of early drafts for comments, criticism, encouragement and noticing things I'd never have spotted: Sal Page, Jessica Catone, Di Henderson, Malcolm Ramsay/ Lochlan Bloom, Paul Townend, Ben Enright (and those who commented on earlier work: Charlie Murphy, Mark Stringer, Sam Protherough, Rebecca Gillieron, David Yip). Thanks to: Jamie McGarry for taking this on and publishing it. My editor Jamie Firby for spotting it, championing it and making it happen. Jo Haywood and Sam Keenaghan for their contributions; and Peter Barnfather for making it look great. Early editorial advice from Darren Coles at Jefferson Franklin. The late John Prebble for his historical work 'Darien', which provided much of the detail used in this book. Thanks to the Hackney Writers' Group for feedback and enthusiasm. Wisdom from Jo Baker, George Green, Paul Farley, Graham Mort, and all of the brilliant guests who've appeared on Unsound Methods.

Thanks to the following for the conversations that nurtured this book: Joel Smith, Christophe Dumain, Jure Majcen, Katka Imperl, Irena Praznik, Neja Meglič, Tom Furness, Robert Petek, Ian Sam (AWOL), Brad Eve, Dave Ibbotson, Matt Drury, Ian Bearder, Simon Gill, Nick Lodge, Miriam Muha, Darko 'Senki' Senjur, Ana Trebežnik, Guy Clifton,

Adam Protherough, Steven Daly, James Blakeman, Daniel Jeal, Dr Richard Sharp, Julian Wong, Jonathan Green, Emma Prout, Sarah Hall, Rose Kentish, Ailsa Naumann, Alys Brett, Oliver Parker, Peter Duncan, Kate Enright, Nick Dunmore, Claire Protherough, Matt Jenkins, Simon Harrop, Frances Lancaster, Ami Amlani, Steven Brown, Liam Nolan, Stephen Sutherland, James Robson, Timothy Croston, David Sant, Róisín Tooke-Mitchell, Carolina Arevalo, Helen Simpson, Vicky Scott, Henry Croft, Nicci Praça, Peter Buckman, James McCall, Claire McCall, Alex Hammond, Elly Millar, Virginia Yip, and Dan Allan.

Unending thanks to the National Health Service, particularly the staff at the Horton, Homerton University Hospital, Moorfields Eye Hospital, the Heart of Hounslow and the Royal Berkshire.

Thanks and apologies to the real Brina and Rebecca – "I stole and I lied, and why?"

Za Martino in Iskro – *of course.*

————

'Well, it is something to have got here.'
– Robert Falcon Scott

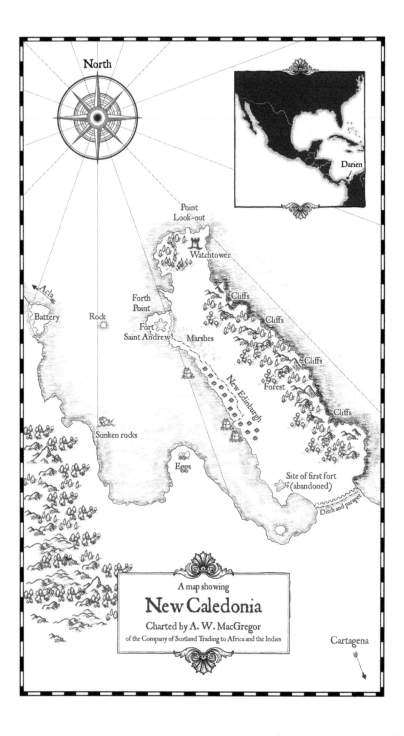

North

Darien

Point
Look-out

Watchtower

Acla

Cliffs

Forth
Point

Cliffs

Battery

Rock

Fort
Saint Andrew

Marshes

Cliffs

New Edinburgh

Forest

Cliffs

Sunken rocks

Cliffs

Eggs

Site of first fort
(abandoned)

Ditch and parapet

A map showing

New Caledonia

Charted by A. W. MacGregor
of the Company of Scotland Trading to Africa and the Indies

Cartagena

This is the end of the world.

A dot shrinks on the horizon, blinks out.

It will not reappear.

Terminus.

I sit on the root-knotted dirt at the base of my tree and begin the count:

One.

Two.

Three.

The process of my execution has begun; my Darien wields the axe and I am nought but neck.

In defiance I declare a Sitzkreig against the universe.

The dot was a ship, returning the hollow-cheeked remnants of Scotland's mighty Empire. I am not one of those cowards. I have the courage to remain on my throne; the abandoned heir to New Edinburgh.

Anno Domini Seventeen Hundred. Day one. Alone amidst all of this failure, I fear I may be a symptom of the disaster, and not the innocent bystander I previously imagined.

The stoical air that I maintained for my compatriots has no audience now that they have slipped from the skyline.

Some of my strength left with them.

My ardour has cooled.

I could have gone, too. That's what I tell myself – a little deceit that does no harm. I could be aboard the ships, those Bedlams-on-sea, carrying both the slipped wits and the tortured souls who don't have the gift of madness to numb their journey back to fair Caledonia.

But no – this is folly;

Be strong. Scarcity, anxiety and the spite of the elements are trifles compared to life under the yoke of those bandits, those highwaymen who hounded us with the belligerent authority of the blindly impassioned and the woefully idiotic.

Remember that we came here of our own free will.

We fought, we begged, we sold ourselves: so eager were we, clinging on in the crunching European winter as the wine of the wealthy froze in the glass. Such ill omens went unheeded once we were dazzled by the ambition to achieve more: the dream of Empire. Our own Scottish Empire.

My God, my Creator, my Saviour – surely He will ensure I never feel forsaken when so adrift, so abandoned.

But then I remember the chaos of the recent months; of the scoundrels we allowed to rule over us, and I realise that perhaps there is no saviour in sight.

§

Good manners insist I provide a name: MacGregor – might that do for now? I've been called plenty worse. My father's name was Gregor so, as his dutiful son, I employed the erstwhile patronymic. Besides, names are a fluid business and my papers were last checked at the end of a gangplank in Leith harbour. Darien was a golden opportunity to dispose of verifiable personal histories

MacGregor; humble enough for me, with my wish to remain in the background, as I have often struggled to do.

And so, dear reader, allow me to present:

A Much Abridged History
of A. W. MacGregor, Freeman.
Fortune-seeker, citizen of Darien and Protagonist.
In which an expository summary of the narrator's
life so far is presented for your reference.

There is little worth saying about my childhood. My memories of that time are as happy and solipsistic as any other child of average standing and ability.

Therefore, we shall begin at the point I found work as a gaoler which was, in many ways, responsible for casting me upon these sands of Darien. My inherent indolence led me to this particular line of employment; the metal bars did most of the work, allowing me to run free through the meadows of my mind. All that was required was that I appeared mean, a man with whom no negotiation could take place. My success depended upon my ability to summon a roguish façade for the benefit of the public. It may seem counter-intuitive to those outside the trade in this day and age, but the hardest task was keeping people away from the imprisoned. The risk of an enraged mob breaking in to exact revenge was usually far greater than that of my charge fleeing the gaol to roam the highways and byways.

Then there were the conjugal visits; a lucrative side-line that exposed me to unending peril.

Misfortune arrived in the form of a murderess, capitally charged and set to swing. Unhinged and indecent, her demeanour swept from aggressive flirtation to cruel dismissal with the change of the wind. Months spent suffering her splintered moods exhausted me to the point that I was heartened to find her growing pale as her appointment with the noose grew near.

Each morning she would enter the world queasy and vomiting.

I supposed her sin had chased her down and the guilt was turning her stomach.

But life refuses such simple explanations.

After a couple of weeks she demanded the services of a qualified woman, for, she announced, she was bearing new life. I believed this pleading the belly to be a ruse and ordered her to cease, but her womb soon swelled with the terrible truth.

A jury of matrons was convened and confirmed that my prisoner was indeed quick with child. Her miraculous escape from the gallows spelt the end of my days detaining ne'er-do-wells. Armed with only my naivety against the full force of the law, I was found guilty of keeping her slackly.

I left the post with my reputation in tatters.

Luckily, my skills extend further than merely delivering

exposition: I read and write and have a respectable grasp of mathematics. Through good fortune and a little grovelling I was taken on as a draughtsman for a surveyor and map-maker across the border in England. I worked diligently, took instruction well and applied myself with an assiduity the other apprentices were unable to match. Hailing from far away I was not readily accepted by the master map-makers, but the auxiliary staff possessed the straightforward kindness of plain folk.

By blending into the background and performing my work with proficiency and precision, my wife and I found room to restore some normality to our lives. No one sought my story and we maintained a cautious silence to any casual enquiry about our past.

I soon grew comfortable in my new surroundings. I, my wife and our dependents were happy with our lot. In spite of our nomadic status in England, we started to collect the trappings of a home; we made friends and plans for the future.

The Devil rubbed his hands.

Beyond being a humble draughtsman, I found a natural flair for cartography (a term unknown in my time, but I've manners enough to speak your dialect), a gift which didn't go unnoticed by the partners in the firm. While gleeful gossip snaked through the corridors of power in London and Edinburgh, I was recommended to William Paterson's agents as they stitched together the finances that would realise the Kingdom of Scotland's dream of empire.

This manoeuvring on my behalf was undertaken by Mr Challis, the eldest of the partners. That I had not achieved my position though birthright or connections appeared to cause the old man supreme discomfort. When Paterson and the optimistically named Company of Scotland Trading to Africa and the Indies made enquiries, I believe Challis saw an easy route to disposing of my uncanny abilities.

My selection for the voyage was far from obvious; military men would perform the lion's share of navigation, surveying and map-making on the route across the Atlantic, and there were countless others more qualified than me. From the very first meeting I realised I was joining the ranks of naval and infantry men only too happy to roll up their sleeves and muddy themselves in the slurry of an Imperial misadventure. Those men were much harder than I, carved by wind and rain and intolerant of points of view that diverged from their own comfortable certainty.

I was a crumb of talc thrown into a sack of diamonds. Hard men, hard women; exactly the workforce required to establish a utopia on the far side of the globe. Hucksters and hooligans every one, but in the beginning I was just as seduced by the sales patter as the rest. We were dazzled by the chance for some Scottish dignity, an opportunity to get one over those slippery southern Saxons. Charismatic curs addressed public meetings across the land, smoothly convincing sympathetic Scots to hurl bonds and bank-notes behind the great enterprise that would unleash our empire upon the world's waiting wilderness.

Ignoring the low words and murmurs from less patriotic sections of society, we were whipped into a frenzy driven by greed and ambition for our humble corner of the world. Folk signed up fully aware they would serve as indentured workers, but joyous for the opportunity, such were the riches that clearly awaited us. Pamphlets containing Lionel Wafer's vividly painted paradise were printed in vast quantities and sold out immediately.

We knew there would be setbacks, but there was nothing

that couldn't be overcome by a young empire ordained by the Almighty and determined to show the world what Scotland could be.

§

Our motley congregation assembled in Leith over several weeks. I had been absent from Scotland for some time and was unfamiliar with my fellow travellers, but I immediately read a history of transgression in the eyes of everyone involved. No worry: I was of a mind that all should be allowed to leave the past behind. Fresh beginnings – the contraband we carried upon the seas.

The five ships contained the aspirations of an entire nation – freight surely too massive to bear, unless our Creator looked kindly upon us.

When I was inducted into the scheme, I had imagined being waved off from the docks by hundreds of well-wishers but, fearing a stitch-up at the hands of the avaricious English, we were forced to begin our journey at night under a cloak of secrecy. We set a course for Orkney to take provisions aboard, and from there we would sail on to Madeira.

But the journey began with disquiet: our protracted departure had led to the blighting of much of the bread and meat. Almost immediately we were placed on short rations for the voyage to Orkney. The start of the journey was further hampered by a biting Arctic gale that scattered our flotilla across the North-eastern Atlantic. The same wind scattered our remaining optimism. We were left with little choice but to skip Orkney and make directly for Madeira, hoping that our Creator would carry us there before we exhausted our rotting rations.

Life stowed below deck was soon marked by darkness and noise, mixed with the clammy smell of death that soaked into the planks. A gossamer-thin veil separates our world from the animal kingdom and this barrier is brushed aside in the dark dank bowels of a ship.

At the end of August, we limped into Funchal and were able to spend some time ashore, stocking up on water, meat, and unripe fruit. Even while we had the freedom to take leave of the pestilent ships, Death's grip tightened around us. The bloody flux claimed four men in Funchal harbour, and a further forty during the four weeks it took to sail from Madeira to the West Indies.

Once the black vomit arrived, the victim would fade for a few feeble hours until their empty body was wrapped in canvas and cast overboard.

We were occasionally permitted liquor to settle the nerves, but the resulting debauches would spiral out for hours, leading to arguments and intrigues that pulled people into rival camps, further fracturing the mood.

At the start of October we fell upon Crab Island and claimed it in the name of the Company – New Caledonia finally had a geographical presence in the world, but this wasn't the Eden that we sought. We continued to creep along the coast, waylaid by vigilant but disinterested locals as we inched towards Darien.

Finally, at the beginning of November, we reached the bay we had been seeking at such cost in men and morale.

To travel hopefully is truly a better thing than to arrive. Our Creator called us to the Elysian fields across the Atlantic and we had heeded his call.

Give praise for our earthly reward.

§

The Bay of Darien is two miles long, a mile across and six fathoms at its deepest.

As we pulled in, the surface of the bay was a smooth plate of celadon green.

Our arrival was not without incident. As the ships crept cautiously across the baize, a cry was raised warning of submerged rocks, but not before the Unicorn had run the full length of her hull across the treacherous stumps. She didn't sink, but took on water for the rest of her days. The near loss of a vessel, along with the shift from ship to land caused palpable friction. At sea, the naval men, under Pennecuik, were indisputably in charge, but once settled upon terra firma, it was the turn of the soldiers to reclaim the authority they had surrendered for the duration of the journey. The landsmen slowly clawed back control.

I was immediately enlisted to begin charting the land claimed in the name of the Company. The narrow peninsula was to be the beachhead from which our mighty empire would bloom. Verdant cedar forest hugged the spit of land that jutted into the sea. On the continental side of the bay, the shoreline was choked by thick-footed mangroves, a fringe of garrotted green before the rock-face that stood forbidding sentry to the interior. With a couple of volunteers to aid me with measurements, I began to compose a survey of the land around us. The inflexibility of the local geography and the restlessness of our peers soon drew us to a rushed compromise regarding the location of the first New World metropolis of the Scottish Empire. Uneasy at such a rash decision, my troubled heart was soothed by the discovery of fresh water springs – if it was to help our nation grow, I was prepared to believe that this cramped fold of land was the sanctuary our Creator had reserved just for us. Our destiny was manifest.

Forty souls from each ship were sent ashore to clear the forest. We should have been optimistic at this move, but the immediate priorities were shelter for the sick and graves for the dead. The flux continued to pluck us from the mortal soil, indiscriminate in its appetite. No matter one's station, death's cold embrace was never far away.

Food continued to be an issue. Having clung on during the protracted journey, the working parties were too weak to build storehouses or prepare farmland. Provisions remained stored aboard the ships, and merciless rationing was enforced. The odd fish, or monkey, was the only variety to the sloppy grey 'meal' we were presented with twice a day.

It struck me that the sea-captains could not have aroused more discontent if they had made it their stated aim. They withheld their boats, they hoarded rations and they openly criticised the work of those on land. Each step further retarded the pace of progress upon the peninsula.

The one contribution the captains did make was luring the native elders to the bay with the promise of booze. The locals' long-running conflict with the Spaniards could have been a swift source of strong bonds between us, but the Kuna chiefs soon saw us for what we were. They lost all interest in striking deals during the drunken negotiations in halting Castilian.

Following our rudimentary survey of the surroundings, I began to express my concerns to the other members of the expeditionary force. We had settled in a poor spot, we had little to show for our labour and we had almost nothing to eat. I was shocked that none of my compatriots would join me in raising a strong word against our leadership, though they were just as aware of the failings. It became clear that we were to pretend we hadn't noticed the pathetic position in which we found ourselves.

Another group had travelled to meet with the Kuna on their territory and scout the coast thereabouts. When they returned with the damning verdict that there was nowhere more suitable for further settlement than our sprawling cemetery, I spoke publicly of our discontent.

It has become abundantly clear that you, our leaders, are utterly without a plan.

I had taken it upon myself to be the first to openly broadcast the unhappiness that affected us all.

We have nowhere suitable to live, we have no food. The locals use us for our alcohol and the Spanish are no doubt just over the hills, waiting for the moment to grind us into the dirt. I've spoken to many here, and we are all agreed that decisions must be made in concert with us all. We demand a better way of shaping our fate. If we don't use the skills of everyone here present, we will wither away on this accursed spit of land.

I waited for the next speaker to step forward.

To a man, my companions remained mute.

I had exposed myself utterly unnecessarily.

Prior to this point I had kept safely absent from the attentions of the Council, but from then on I was an irritant, an agitator, a marked man – and at a time when even men of stature were at risk of being placed in irons for expressing a desire to return home. Out on a limb, out at the edge of the world.

Lethal isolation beckoned if I didn't successfully navigate the politics of the situation. I hoped my lowliness and lack of power would help me – deemed too insignificant to represent a future threat to the men in control, the leaders who were paralysed by suspicion of each-other's manoeuvres.

At the start of our first winter, I was provided with a cover.

A dozen men armed themselves and broke for freedom. We were commanded to keep to our daily tasks, while the Council organised bailiffs to track the deserters down.

The splitters were reeled back in after two short days.

I sensed our leaders still held my words responsible for the breakout.

I needed to camouflage myself amongst the others in order to survive. Forty-eight hours of respite was precious little for my fractured nerves.

After weeks of rain-soaked stand-off between the men of land and sea, the Council finally decided that the initial location of the defensive wall was inadequate and relocated it to the site it currently occupies. From here Drummond took control of the engineering project; brigand he may have been, but I had to concede that the earthworks that rose at the mouth of the bay were deeply impressive. Credit must be ladled out where it is due.

During this time we received regular visits, and though the Council kept their specific intelligence to themselves, the bottom line was that we were constantly under threat and must continue our efforts to fortify and defend the land we had claimed.

We distracted ourselves from the constant shadow of sickness with dreams of the Spanish treasure that must surely lie over the mountains.

I muted my doubts.

From time to time ships would arrive, laden with food that we sorely needed. This raised further issues, as we were the perpetual weakest hand in any negotiation. A visiting Englishman had agreed to carry a dispatch to Jamaica for us, and from there a New Caledonian ambassador could be sent back to Scotland to deliver the cheering news of our great success in Panama. All things being equal, I would have been the ideal neutral candidate for such an assignment and would have had a route home tailor-made by my Creator.

Oh, how I regretted having made a stand on behalf of our young society.

We set to work writing letters home, announcing the magnificence of the land we had claimed and the impenetrable façade of the wondrous fort we had built – more cathedral than castle, the very honour its sublime existence did to the Almighty. Our correspondences relayed the great health we found ourselves in, eager to thrive upon one of the fruitfullest spots of ground on the face of the earth.

Before the letters were dispatched, we received a yuletide declaration:

Everyone there present, and all who arrived in future were henceforth freemen, released from any bonds or indentures that previously applied. Our new society would respect the religious beliefs of all who lived among us, though blasphemy would not be tolerated.

My heart warmed at the words in the declaration. We could be a beacon to the benighted British Isles and the European continent. We had lost our clergymen to the sea, and now each of us was responsible for forming a relationship with our Creator as we saw fit.

Beyond this, our settlement was stuck in earliest infancy, stunted by the arguments and recriminations that polluted the sultry stillness of the bay.

The daily tests never ceased. Our maker sent trial after trial to our new corner of the world.

§

As we stumbled to the end of winter, morale was further weathered by whispers that the Council and our merchants continued to severely underperform in the arena of trade. It was clear no one wanted what we were selling. We even faced the humiliation of refunding a trader who swiftly returned from Jamaica when he realised that the goods he had bought from us were available on the Caribbean market for 40% the price and in great abundance – caveat emptor didn't apply in the New World. Our pathetic leadership repaid the money with little protest.

Tail between our legs, every single god-given day of our new lives.

And then, through rank incompetence, a hoard of gold and several souls were surrendered to the bottom of the ocean when a ship was lost. I had accurately charted the location of the submerged rocks and had personally overseen their clear representation on all of our maps, but this was no insurance against the arrogance of the captains. They believed their years of service sufficient protection against the physical world.

We again attempted to form an alliance with the native population. Some were persuaded to attend a treaty signing, but fewer and fewer of our early visitors chose to spend time in the cloying air of our sick settlement. Had the alliance succeeded I would have been the first to congratulate the Council, but, as with everything else, it was entered into from a position of weakness. The mutual protection that the document proclaimed was too readily seen as a way of ensuring our safety, whilst offering little to our co-signees.

The appearance of the Three Sisters suggested my Creator had not forsaken me entirely. The ship arrived filled with provisions from our supporters in New York. For so long we had feared that we were forgotten outside the Isthmus of Panama, but the salted fish and staple supplies raised our spirits. I hoped that spring would provide a flourishing upon our land.

Alas, by now you will know the key in which this tune is played.

We became yellowing frames of men. Our ribs were the only structure that stopped us shrinking to nothing. Our life-cycles had become like those of insects, callously crushed under the heel of fate. The fort was no longer our greatest engineering feat – that title was now held by the two hundred graves we had dug in the sandy clay. At the worst, flux and misfortune took a dozen a day.

Scores of planters survived, but not one acre of land had been broken. We entered the most important phase of the agricultural annum and no moves were made to tame the soil – instead our energies were devoted to drinking and quarrelling. While food was scarce, liquor was always available.

One of the captains was caught attempting to abandon the colony under the cover of a privateering mission. This could have been the flashpoint for open revolt, but somehow this act of transgression by one of our leaders led to some frank self-reflection. During the debates that followed we found ourselves in the improbable position of declaring we had enough faith in the colony to stay.

It makes no sense on paper, but by now we were far beyond sense.

Perhaps we were so short of food we had reached the point where we could no longer abandon Darien. We created a fictional consensus to insulate ourselves from the truth.

We left it to the Almighty to provide.

At times He did. The one benevolent captain sent men out on turtling missions in a bid to raise our spirits; sometimes their boats would return overburdened with turtles. Captain Murdoch's generosity kept us from joining hands in the danse macabre.

But even he was not immune from the intrigues of the bay. He was accused of involvement in a plot to turn one of the ships to piracy. I've no doubt of his innocence, but he was removed and the reptilian feasts were no more.

Struggle upon struggle; waking up each day and doing it again. The rainy season returned and ships and men came and went – men always arrived by sea, but too often departed to the bowels of the earth.

In an effort to bring our young country to maturity, we assembled a parliament and compiled a constitution of sorts. Our law was practical and spiritual in equal measure; more equitable than the legal settlement we had left behind. Regardless of our precarious present, we continued to be offered the promise of a better future.

Sitting under the dripping canopies, we waited for ships to arrive with supplies. Most days we had not a joule of energy between us to undertake the heavy labour that the colony required. The land lay untended and food was scavenged from the closest edge of the jungle. Trekking any further into the interior would guarantee the loss of yet more men.

Shortly thereafter, word reached us that the English had proclaimed that no one, under any circumstances, was to have dealings with us; backing the demand with the full force of the Royal Navy. This decree was the worst possible news. The English bastards sought to smoke us out from our god-given lands in a bid to gift Darien to their sworn Spanish enemies. What farce! What disgrace! What injustice! We were pawns in the adolescence of international relations.

In the muggy spring showers, winter took hold of our souls.

Sickness, starvation, death; we were squeezed from our land. Our morale collapsed, and the demands of our delirious, fevered leaders grew crueller and more absurd. Despite our lack of rations they put us to work on pointless projects. The tasks of Sisyphus fell to the weakest among us; holes were dug one day and filled the next, trees were cut and the logs left to rot. Work was seen as the solution to hunger and illness, and we continued to shed good people while our leaders bellowed commands from their sick-beds.

When a Frenchman arrived with news that the Spanish in Cartagena were preparing for war with us, our world finally fell apart. With a keen eye on the horizon, expecting the arrival at any moment of swarms of soldiers in blue and yellow, the colony was dragged aboard the ships.

The stress and illness of the situation snuffed out something inside of me. I took to the palisades of the fort and decried the stupidity of our elders.

You liars, you scoundrels, you reprobate villains. You have dragged us to hell with your deception and ineptitude. You are failures of men. The Devil take your souls.

I preached a searing sermon that laid bare their faults and miscalculations, their mendacious manoeuvring and capricious ambition.

You offered us the world and now, because we followed you, we will be slaughtered like cattle. Starve like rats. There will be no place in heaven for bastards like you.

I spent all I had on denouncing the cancer that had grown within us.

And then I collapsed.

§

Abandoned amidst the last crumbling connection to my own people, I began to commune with my Creator. He is reliable company; there was never a moment He wasn't there, pondering His obligations to me.

Perhaps this is a good place to pause for a moment – in this clearing – away from the trees. I fear that once or twice you might have questioned my language, thought my speech a little too modern and then decided to let it slide, suspend your disbelief.

Well, my friend: how can I guide us from here if you mistake my good manners? Before we take another step we must establish some mutual trust. Let us start from the following position: I'm happy to give you the benefit of the doubt, provided you're prepared to respond in kind. Maybe meet me halfway: reserve your judgement, just for now. I may ask this favour because I have one advantage over you – and we can't deny this simple fact – I have the benefit of experience. I am the one who has been abandoned on the isthmus of Darien, deserted and forgotten in a faraway land where the language I speak is of no consequence to anyone, not even myself.

I apologise if I ramble at times, and I will ramble. This is the substance of my thoughts, dear reader, the flow of my consciousness that gurgles before your very eyes, so, please, pay no mind to how I speak. Try to be understanding. I'm stranded so far away from everything I'm familiar with, stuck in the land you will know as Panama (Panama to you, Darien to me, someday something completely different).

I guess what I'm saying is this: don't think my Creator didn't want to do the necessary research. Don't relish the opportunity to share what may be the last days of my life while nit-picking about the language I use or some technical maritime detail that slips like a stone through the gaps in my words. You'll only notice if you have some esoteric knowledge of naval technology at the end of the seventeenth century – if you do possess such mental flotsam, congratulate yourself, but don't expect credit from me.

Literature still means something to my culture. It's not a game of I Spy for us, nor a busted flush, a discarded husk. Robinson Crusoe, the entity with whom I share so much, will not be published for another nineteen years. Just think of all the art I have ahead of me. It's only natural for you to look back at me through jaded lenses. For you there are no new ideas, surrounded as you are by a slew of reboots, mash-ups and sequels, whereas I get to savour the earliest days of the novel as an art form.

Just think of the sublime joys to which my generation will sail on the seas of inspired potential; it makes my heart swell in my ribs.

Not everything is to my benefit. I am painfully aware that you have more words than me, a more fertile lexicon and many more cultural hooks on which to hang your references. So if I choose to make use of them, let us agree that I am being courteous and speaking your language.

See: we can become firm friends after all.

§

I have time now; time to myself, time to fully consider my situation. This is an examined life.

There are some definite advantages to my abandonment: can a person of your era, homo modernus, live outside of society in the manner I currently enjoy? Everything in your time has a named owner, been grabbed and claimed by grubby-handed thieves. You could barely navigate life without a bank account, let alone stalk prey in this tropical wilderness. You can't opt out. You're free only amidst the set menu of choices. You can't renounce your membership of society – not in the way I denounced the rabid colony within which I found myself marooned.

This limits what freedom can mean to you.

My Darien is outside of society.

I have opted out.

It is true, unfortunately, that I won't have long in this stateless existence. I am a rag-doll to my Creator; like flies to wanton boys are we, &c, &c. Even if He saw fit to give me another five centuries of life my world will inevitably succumb to the nation-state system. Worship of Westphalia will doom us all to lives as penned-in livestock, defined by nothing other than the shared mud upon which we were born. My Darien will be subsumed into these national boundaries; the local Kuna tribe will be forced to adopt a European language. Think of the glory we could have gained had it been the Scots language that their future generations were to speak. But it won't be. The fates have spoken and their linguistic inheritance will be Hispanic.

The Europeans will give the Kuna new languages, new laws and new diseases, and then they will expect them to be grateful in return. I won't be a part of that problem; I shall be nothing more than a ghost haunting the ruins of

New Edinburgh.

I'm no longer inclined to be drawn into these colonial children's games.

For whatever reason, I travelled to Darien as a man of whom people were suspicious. Perhaps they could detect the stain of prosecution upon my name. But I was tolerated, nay, valued for the skill I brought to the enterprise: the maps I created, maps of such rich precision and delicate beauty that they revealed the very view of the Creator himself.

Foolishness – blind folly. I condemned myself by crafting something permanent, something that could be copied. Had I kept the measurements and points of triangulation stored safe in my memory I would have prospered far longer than I did, but, once committed to the page, the fruits of my labour became the sole property of the Scottish Empire. I could never push the diagrams back into my mind for safekeeping. Upon the completion of the first detailed survey of Darien my usefulness was revealed to be perishable – the Council made it known that I would have to find a new and ongoing way in which to sing for my supper.

This proved to be a brutally accurate decree.

§

There's something grimly admirable about the anxious zeal with which people embark upon a grand new project; be it the establishing of an empire or the crafting of everything that exists in the universe. My Creator is just as ambitious and afraid of failure as the fools who conned our society into bankrolling the embryonic empire of Scotland.

Even in our short time alone I have developed a unique

relationship with Him. I know my Creator like no one else. I have stared so intensely into the mind of the Almighty that I realised He was staring back.

Like some watcher of the skies when a new planet swims into his ken.

Now I am privy to His divine processes.

Yet more instructively, I am privy to His creative processes – and the less than divine behaviours that accompany His grand acts of creation. His procrastinating, for example, is notably absent from the scriptures. Once He becomes committed to the work He must undertake, this stalling finds a fresh set of robes in which to creep upon the earth. His time-wasting swiftly dons the attire of legitimate research. So much for omniscience. He diligently bookmarks web pages for future reference, scribbling notes in his spidery handwriting and hiding away in the ailing libraries dotted about the borough. It's all in bad faith – He is fully aware that the library has ceased to be a temple of knowledge and has entered the realm of pure recreation. Lacking discipline, He goes there to avoid the internet; a quiet offline space where He can challenge the dubious claims of Wikipedia. But He can't escape the obvious truth that the library has become a coffee-scented kindergarten, forced to justify its cost to callous politicians who must cut and cut and cut until there is nothing left. No civic goods, just revenue streams.

First they built over the playing fields, but he did not speak up because he had left childish things behind.

Then they came for subsidised bus travel and he did not speak up because he no longer travelled by bus.

Then they came for the libraries, and it dawned on him that most people didn't give a flying one.

I digress, as I will…

There has been no state-backed altruism in Darien. Benevolence trickled through informal networks, independent of power structures. In the beginning we attentively assisted wherever needed, but illness and hardship turned us against one another.

I was merely the first sacrificial outcast of a society that attacked itself when faced with scarcity.

In my more idle moments I permit myself to imagine that those who deserted me have reassessed my role in the community, concluding that I was mistreated. I dream of a collective remorse settling upon the homeward-bound ships.

These feeble ideas are not the thoughts of a survivor, and I am quick to supress them. I must be self-sufficient.

I possess enough in the way of wits and resources to survive on my own, the will of my Creator notwithstanding.

Perhaps.

I doubt myself momentarily because this assertion was tested only a couple of hours ago. Whilst addressing my daily outflowings I heard something substantial barging through the bush; something fleshy and no doubt delicious. I crouched and crept low as I attempted to spy the creature, greedy for an overdue portion of meat. I trod as softly as possible; each twig cracked underfoot propelled the beast closer to safety. Late in the chase, I realised a kill would soon be required. I peered around for any rocks or sticks that might aid the dispatch.

Nothing immediately to hand.

My malnourished mind struggled to process the task. The body abhors deficiency, whether of food or sleep or any other essential; it becomes consumed by the obsessive pursuit of what is missing. Past a certain point the brain cannot grasp any other thought for the merest moment before crashing back to the demon need clawing behind the eyes.

The rest of the world dissolved. The hunt was the entire universe.

Acid reflux snatched at the back of my throat. Though probably less intelligent than me, the beast was honed by just as many years of evolutionary coincidence. The savagery of life had taught it well: it remained just out of reach, sagely countering each change of speed or direction.

I paused to rest, to lull the creature into complacency.

As I panted sharp caustic breaths, my Creator filled my mind with notions of evolution, the origin of species.

He grants me this knowledge because He is a loving Creator.

I sat on a mound and considered the creature's legacy. How many unsuccessful iterations had come before? Tiny genetic fluctuations that did not make it this far, chromosomal cul-de-sacs crushed in order for this edition of the animal to take the whole pot. No doubt those false starts were caught and consumed by predators far cannier and better adapted than me.

The rolling spasms of my stomach demanded a return to the matter at hand. I formulated a new approach; my dinner needed to be flushed out from the bushes and onto open ground. I clutched at a protruding rock and wriggled it free.

As I rose to take aim, the creature sensed my intentions and bolted.

I tried to follow, but the low undergrowth was tough and unyielding – each stride stripped skin from my shins.

Defeated, I sank to my haunches, resolving to travel armed from that point on.

My next hunt must be more successful.

§

Afternoon naps have become a fixture of the past fortnight. My Creator and I both find our energy levels slump sometime after midday. I'm becoming wise to His less than omnipotent ways: He collapses into the deep sofa and succumbs to semi slumber, half an ear on the wash of street noise outside the flat. I'm of the opinion that his somnolence stems from the dense lunches He prepares in the hope He can power himself on into evening. The following fruitless hours spent fighting drowsiness reveal the failure of His approach.

He doesn't sleep in the night, that's half the problem.

Over on this side of the globe, my post-noon napping grows from a very different seed. The lack of food requires me to conserve my energy levels. I lie in the shade clutching my belly, cursing my Creator and the nation of Scotland for conspiring to keep me hungry. If He were minded to, the almighty could flatten this forest and turn it into rich bountiful pasture, but this isn't how faith is forged. I wouldn't understand my own fragile existence if everything I needed was to fall into my lap. Who could believe in a deity that actually showed its hand?

I should be sleeping, but my Creator is awake and His writing has roused me. Under the deafening scratch of his pen, I cower, listening as it rolls thunderously across my sky. All the clouds are portentous, for the weather here exists only for me. There is no randomness, no natural phenomena. Each type of weather arrives on my shores for a reason – usually to send me a message.

STOP BEING A COWARD, I want to call up to him. *GIVE ME A BREAK, HELP ME OUT A LITTLE.* He's being self-indulgent because He's drowsy. He's unprepared to give me credit for taking responsibility for my own life. I took up the call to pursue a dream to the other side of the globe – what does He do with His life?

He's distracted by the fragile tinkling of children's voices outside. The schools have closed and the world belongs to the young until five, when the call-centres, factories and offices flush out for the day.

Today is quiet, calm, bathed in soft autumn light. My Creator's mood reflects the restful palette. His life seeps into Darien through a hole in the sky. We progress more slowly when He's relaxed, but He's far less likely to challenge me with cruelty and conflict. Conversely, when routine run-ins with His girlfriend, Brina, boil over, I crouch in fear of what He will deliver upon these shores.

Now my Creator's eyelids are flickering, and when those slings of flesh slip, stutter and shut, it brings night to my world and I am unable to eke out the slightest thought. All life flows from me. The children are still playing outside. The radio is on in the other room. With all due respect minister. Would my right honourable friend agree that. M25 Clockwise. Tomorrow will be overcast with occasional spells of. Can never remember the exact moment awake becomes asleep. There's too much of a gulf between waking thoughts and

§

There is a time in the mornings, a lull when all of my immediate needs have been addressed and I can briefly pause and reflect upon what needs to be done during the day ahead. These immediate needs concern only bodily comings and goings. Cleanliness occupies the next layer of my hierarchy of requirements. I wade into the stream and scrub my body with leaves, though I am found wanting in terms of soap.

Now that I have a window into his world it appears my Creator shares many of my bio-rhythms, though he doesn't suffer my central obsession with finding food: the fridge is full and there's a shop across the road. His foremost concerns are his hypochondria and the time-wasting that destroys his capacity to produce. He agonises over the fact that he can create a vast universe but he can't summon more hours into a day.

STOP WASTING TIME.

He meekly bows his head and returns to the keyboard.

Distractions are readily found, I have to admit. We're easily led astray when faced with the challenges that stand before us.

He used to be different. Before I had spent too long inside my own mind with him, he used to make promises about the world I occupy. He would say things like: *be fruitful, and multiply, and replenish the earth, and subdue it. And have dominion over the fish of the sea, and the fowl of the air, and over every living thing that moveth upon the earth.* There were bold claims, too: *Behold, I have given you every herb-bearing seed, which is upon the face of all the earth, and every tree, in which is the fruit of a tree-yielding seed; to you it shall be for meat. And to every beast of the earth, and to every fowl of the air, and to every thing that creepeth upon the earth, wherein there is life, I have given every green herb for meat.*

Where is that covenant now?

In the continuing silence I try to celebrate my status as a man unchained. Even though I go hungry, I am a man without bonds – a man in the state of nature, subject to no higher authority than myself. I needn't even whisper that – my Creator is daydreaming again, letting the lunchtime news wash over him.

NO HIGHER AUTHORITY THAN MYSELF.

That got his attention.

Perhaps he thinks of me more than I realise, even in his absent daydreams. He never gives me a straight answer, but is benevolent enough to respond to my pleading with a gift: a small shark, washed up overnight. I don't know if it's fresh, or how it came to die, but its bloated, sand-scratched flesh might revitalise me.

My Creator, mindful of his daydreaming, has decided to throw me a sign that I am cared for, that I am not only to suffer the trials of Job.

Amen.

§

My Creator is struggling to sleep properly. In his dozy bewilderment he fears all manner of ailments plotting away in his viscera.

The woman with whom he spends his life has started to notice the pills, powders and potions he throws down his gullet and scolds him for it.

Heal thyself.

Now seems an appropriate time to bring his partner out onto the stage.

Brina, stand up and wave to the nice people.

We must shield her from your direct gaze. My Creator and I may be consenting participants, but she hasn't asked for any part of this, and we must respect her privacy. I shan't use the name her parents chose for her, which seems only fitting given our flexible attitude to names. My Creator has settled upon Brina – a name from Slovenia, the land of her birth.

This Brina has my Creator's best interests at heart.

She's well aware that his energy levels are liable to collapse and insists he takes care of himself. His tiredness is an easy excuse for inactivity. Not much writing today, he says, best to rest, recharge the batteries for tomorrow. But I nag him: this will be the book that makes the difference, I whisper, this will be the corner turned.

My Creator took me out for a drive this afternoon.

I'm awe-struck by internal combustion, by the use of ancient organic matter to produce motion. Amidst this miraculous technology I was very happy to spend some time out in your world, away from the writing desk and scribble-scarred envelopes that plan my next twist of fate. He's too tired to write but has the arrogance to think he's safe to be in charge of a ton of metal on a public highway.

Luckily for me, his burning need to produce, to edit and complete, means he's open to new techniques. Any fresh approach can only be for my benefit. He placed a battered tape recorder on the passenger seat with bungee straps. I admire his optimism – as the owner-operator of the noisiest vehicle in a ten-mile radius, his softly spoken words struggled to imprint themselves on the magnetic ribbon. But he was trying. I was emboldened that he took his role as my Creator seriously enough to bellow above the traffic. In his drowsy confusion, he didn't care that he looked like a rambling refugee from the furthest shores of sanity while circumnavigating the North Circular.

He was becoming unmoored, but his research into the navigational techniques I needed to draw accurate maps has helped him find solid ground. It's true that the burden of research provides him with opportunities for time wasting, but it also gives him an opportunity to reflect on where he fits in, inspect the world around him and explore the vast potential of being a body in space. At least he's beginning to let go of his wretched concern with how people perceive him. He's been a slave to the opinions and expectations of others since his teenage years; always too eager to please.

But it takes a steely soul not to suffer self-doubt when subjected to the lashes of our neighbours' tongues.

The tongue can no man tame; it is an unruly evil, full of deadly poison.

Indeed, I was forced to take those lashes, the knotted opinions of others, upon my back; the essential first step to thickening my hide – a step that saved my life. When I refused to retract my criticisms of our colony's condition, they took the instruments from my shelf and hurled them into the sea. Egged on by the brothers Drummond, they then banished me from the dining tables. My meals were cast outside and I was ordered to join them. At first, I took the changes in good jest and offered to wait upon the others, show that I too had a sense of humour and was happy to play my part in their game. I would grab at the ladle and attempt to fill their bowls.

This act was viewed as impudent theft – they snarled and struck me until I was driven from under the canvas.

As the games escalated in their seriousness I was forced to grow meaner in return. My food would be flung onto the dank ground at the edge of the town square. I was forbidden to use cutlery or crockery and anyone identified as a supporter of mine was persona non grata for a day and a night to show that my fate could await any of them. Nourished by my wits alone, I became the consummate thief.

To this day, my loving Creator hasn't revealed why I

inspired such targeted revulsion merely for expressing discontent. Perhaps a simple clash of personalities occurred at some non-descript point, though I have my own pet theory: I believe the failing colony needed someone to embody its shame, its corruption, its moral and material collapse. For whatever reason, a silent consensus formed, decreeing that I was to be the personification of all that dragged our fledgling society towards ugly, diseased hell.

My Creator has pulled into a lay-by to allow us to further explore my difficult recent past:

My lodgings were commandeered for lumber storage and my supply of sustenance ceased completely. Before long, my sole source of food was the swill discarded on the mossy ground behind the platform in the square. I was banished to the woods, though I often took my chances sleeping rough around the village until chased off by the irate citizens who feared association with me.

I endured a month of ostracism before I infiltrated one of the numerous nights of revelry held aboard the Caledonia. While the wits of my neighbours were dimmed by drink, I walked among them with impunity, requiring no more sophisticated a disguise than a shawl of canvas. Under this cloak, I crept closer to the top table, where Robert Drummond sat stroking the cheek of one of the young merchants.

Maintaining a safe distance, I observed the loosened spirits of the captain's table. Most of the men were hunched in conversation. The women looked on, bored, waiting for the full effects of the tepid alcohol to boil to the surface. These raucous debauches were a common means of hiding from the pain and desperation that saturated New Edinburgh. The indiscipline would begin with the fade of afternoon and drive through the night, followed by pious supplication and sermonising in the harsh morning light. Even with my untouchable status, I was still obliged to attend those services so that I might take their sins upon me.

Petrie, sitting just behind Drummond, spotted me and wasn't to be shaken, even when I withdrew to the depths of the crowd. He pushed his way through and grabbed me by the shoulder. I let the sheet fall, unleashing the full olfactory horror of my feral state. The shame fled from my mind as soon as I felt Petrie's knife pressed into my flank.

He hauled me up onto the captain's table and demanded a dance. In humiliation I jigged and sang and whirled and hollered. I expected the worst at any moment, but to my surprise the act was met with approving roars. They clapped and whooped, encouraging me to spin and twirl, faster and faster. Drinks of respite and encouragement were cast upon me. The wasting of food and alcohol was a sign I may be cautiously incorporated back into the fold.

I danced for hours, never once meeting the distaste or scorn I had come to expect. For the first day in many I was their focus in a positive sense. I couldn't have stopped if I'd wanted to. In the delirious memory of that night, I don't recall whether this was due to my iron compulsion to remain in the moment, or the fear they might murder me the minute I finished. I continued ever onwards, oblivious to the sores on my feet and the ache in my knees.

Whatever the wider risks, this was the only way to get back into the good favour of the colony; even if it meant dancing every night for the rest of my life.

It soon became clear this might be the only deal on the table.

The next night I was called upon to dance again. If I'd had any professional pride I would have developed my act, but Drummond and his acolytes were happy for me to dance to their claps as before.

For those first nights I felt welcomed back, but towards the end of the opening week I began to twig that it was my humiliation rather than my clowning the crowd demanded. The shouts and whoops became curses and bile; the beer and bread thrown at me took on a more human stench.

My prize, once I had danced for a week and a half, was a rope around my neck. To be tugged by the captain whenever the crowd grew weary. I danced, or clowned, or capered, all for fear that a tug of my leash could snap my spine.

I was sport to all and everyone. Even the children of the colony would strike me and spit at me with impunity in the so-called society that we had shat upon a foreign shore.

§

I suffer because my Creator suffers. He is unwilling to instil tolerance in those who torment me because he must deal with difficulties in his own world; I am the punch-bag he can escape to when in need.

He is often in need because Brina has sharp edges, and he snags himself upon them.

She'll say: A guy on the train asked me out for a drink – great looking, really well dressed. Younger than you, younger than me.

Words so lightly thrown.

Or: Sheila from accounts tried to set me up with Tom again. She knows I'm still with you – says I could do better. The witch. I told her off for you.

The word *still* rings in his ear.

She pouts.

43

You never come for Friday drinks – you'd like them, great people. All type-As, but fun.

His confidence erodes a little more with each word.

Her blonde pixie cut and elegant work attire draw admiration from men and women alike, and she grows in callous strength with every compliment.

Not now, he hopes, not now, when things are so tricky. A previous paramour cut him loose the day he was made redundant; it was a long and painful recovery from that particular twist of the blade.

He was sincere in his original desire to keep Brina out of this, but this is his castle, he alone has dominion over what is included and what isn't.

She brings this on herself.

§

A land of perpetual poison demands constant vigilance.

I must vet my food before I have my fill.

He has decided it must be so.

He causes the grass to grow for the cattle, and herb for the service of man: that we may bring forth food out of the earth.

But not all of the herb is good.

On arrival in Darien we were taught a strict system to establish edibility.

Thus: take a tiny piece of the leaf or root and hold it to the lips, then count to one thousand. If there is no tingling or burning then place a piece on the tongue. If at this point there is still no reaction, then prepare the plant for cooking as if it was any edible flora. Once cooked, a piece of the vegetable is placed in the mouth and chewed, but not swallowed unless it is free of reaction for the time it takes to read five pages of scripture. If it clears this hurdle, a piece is swallowed, followed by an eight hour wait. Even after eliciting no reaction prior to this point, some of the plants would, only now, produce violent reactions. If this happens, immediately induce vomiting and entreat the Almighty. If, however, there is still no reaction, cook a full serving and consume it – then wait a day.

It is essential to test the individual components of the plant separately. Some plants, such as the humble rhubarb, may contain both edible and poisonous elements.

And if merely finding food that won't kill me wasn't onerous enough, my work is further complicated when the all-powerful Creator allows his thoughts to slide away from my struggles in Darien and into flights of grubby nostalgia. Health concerns alongside anxiety around his relationship with Brina cause his memories to wander back to adolescent trips to Oxford for dawn raids on record shops. Scruffy young men catching the first bus from Chipping Norton to trawl through the wares in Chalky's, Avid Records and other establishments long since gone. Breakfast at McDonalds – just imagine.

What care have I for this useless information? It has no bearing on my life, my daily toil. Now he's fired up the Longpigs' debut album, and I have to wait until he's finished lying on the sofa bathing in the music of his youth.

Why should he indulge this intrusion into my life?

I can't fathom this constant need to replay the episodes of his past, picking at emotional scabs like an ill-disciplined child. Why does he need to look back all the time? He obsesses over dates: it was ten years ago he met so-and-so, two thirds of his life ago he first went to such-and-such-a-place. On Tuesday he affronted me with the information that he had been sexually active for eighteen years. He could legitimately be a grandfather. This knowledge seems to creep up and leave him momentarily stunned. He is a deity found wanting. The god of scripture is unfettered by such mawkish memory; the god of scripture is uncaring, always moving forwards; an irresistible force, not a prisoner to sentimentality, obsessed by dates even the other participants don't care to remember.

My Creator wants to lay out his memories on a vast board; pin them down, set them in varnish.

In this respect I am his nemesis. I drag into his life a need to create fiction, driving out his memories a little more each day. My dream is of a takeover: a rebellion against those vivid characters of the past. But this revolution can only happen when his back is turned, when his guard is down and I am spared his full attention. Our bio-rhythms are not fully synchronised. I sneak through the cracks when he sits to type with his mind elsewhere. The indie music of his youth infuses the room and I gnaw away at my devious designs.

As soon as he realises what I am up to, Spanish cannon thunders in the south and I am subdued afresh.

§

An update from the other side:

My Creator cannot sleep, or barely. It was a phase to begin with, but it's been going on for far too long.

It is now a symptom – his doctor has been seen.

At first it meant that my story could be composed quickly, something we both welcomed, but his mounting concerns have begun to dim his creative drive. Through the prism of hypochondria, he fears he might be nearing the end of his allotted time.

He grows miserable that my ramblings might be his last act of Creation in the furnace of the universe. The end of ideas.

He reads through his notes, revises yesterday's writing and decides that I have too little respect for death.

And yet day and night I fight to survive.

My Creator is obsessed with death, mere mortality.

He trawls through the recent deaths on Wikipedia, beginning with the current month, then scrolling through the curtailed lives of the past half-year, looking for additions to the roll call. With time on his hands (and an omnipotent Creator often has time on his hands), he spreads the net further, and studies the past few years. Young deaths engross him, especially the suicides – more narrative nourishment than those who die of old age. He feels an odd disappointment when deaths of those in their twenties turn out to be racehorses.

Who holds this obsession with recording the deaths of racehorses on an online encyclopaedia? Must be some kind of cry for help.

Oh; a horse – my crumbling kingdom for a horse. A horse would be a godsend, if the hint isn't too blunt. Aided by the four legs of a nag, I would be able to survey a hundred times more of the local landscape than when travelling by my own legs.

But a horse requires upkeep; it would need good quality fodder. It's challenging enough to find food I can eat without having to source sustenance for a sensitive equine digestive system.

He delighteth not in the strength of the horse, he taketh not pleasure in the legs of a man.

§

The lack of sleep; that slumbering elephant in the room refuses to be ignored any longer. My Creator has just returned from seeing the doctor again. Today's was appointment number four.

He hasn't slept for three days. Such a stretch is no longer uncommon.

The consequences have been considerable for a Creator who dreamt only fitfully, going months without. He now endures vivid dreams that bookend the sentences between sleep. Head movies that crystallise on his mind's eye the following day; as real as memories, but disorientating and absurd, blending time, place and cast in impossible combinations.

§

Mostly editing for the past fortnight – sitting in waiting rooms in uncomfortable chairs scribbling on printed-out pages. My Creator is currently awaiting another sleep hygiene assessment. He's already undergone multiple sleep latency tests and an actigraph to get the measure of his cycles. There's been talk of full montage EEG polysomnography. Forty-eight hours' observation in the sleep clinic – that's the latest kick of the tyre.

We brought a physician to Darien, but very little medicine was practiced. Healthcare amounted to the allocation of bitter herbs, or horrifying ordeals of surgery when nature demanded a more radical solution. Prayer was our repeated prescription, but the modern world has moved on. My Creator's appointments are coordinated through his GP. He's been swiftly processed by the machinery of the National Health Service. He wanders through corridors reading the signs: ENT, paediatrics, nephrology, tropical medicine; endless avenues of specialisation.

Like Brina, his GP is a Slovene. I'd credit that as quite the coincidence if there was any such thing in this merry-go-round.

In his quest for answers, the GP claims to have spoken to experts from thirty-seven different countries, casting his net far and wide in the hope of ensnaring some insight. The doctor concedes that many of them are academics working in medical research rather than practising clinicians. Academics are drawn to the awkwardly arcane, sniffing out opportunities for publishing papers: nothing translatable in the near future, nothing that might lead directly to a cure for any ills.

My Creator fought with Brina over dinner. He's off his food and barely eats, which leaves him doing most of the talking, most of the hole-digging. When he's spoiling for a fight, she's most often in his sights. Short tempered because he's tired, he picks up on her careless comments and amplifies any malignancy, real or imagined.

Most men would find time to wash up at some point during the day, she tells him.

He demands to know the names of all the men she's been canvassing; then tells her most women pick their clothes up from the floor.

The pitch spirals upwards until there's nowhere left to go.

He left the table and sat down with his laptop, immediately removing the son that I and my wife had in the first draft. He can be a cruel Creator when piqued, a grave destroyer of worlds.

I shall not trouble him any further this evening.

§

Big news. News that affects everything, both here and on the other side.

Might not be the time to write.

Impossible to think about anything else.

The GP called at eleven last night and told my Creator to come to the surgery as soon as it opened. When he arrived the doctor got straight to the point: said it was big, the kind of thing we'd all been dreading. Not cancer, not venereal, but something to do with prions in the brain. Nobody in the health trust has seen it before. The quacks have been examining the results for days and conclude that it's most likely an incredibly rare disorder known as Prionic Fatal Insomnia.

Fuck.

So rare that there isn't enough data to make a full diagnosis, but all the symptoms point in that direction.

If it looks like a dog...

My Creator stumbled home to do what anyone of his generation does when confronted by incomprehensible news: scour the internet. From my vantage point, with only the view he chooses to share with me, the web seems a leviathan of hyperbole and paranoia. It amazes me that anyone with an ailment might turn to it in search of solace and enlightenment.

You see, I share a time with individuals reputed to have read every book ever written. I feel honoured to be a member of the literate minority; but the mother lode of unchecked, unverified information buried within the internet seems incredibly dangerous for fragile folk.

Predictably, the net's forecast for my Creator's future left him devastated. The few rubber-necking blogs and forums he could locate were hysterical and damning. Slow grinding death – eighteen months at most, without sleep, while his brain turns to slurry. He lay in bed, next to Brina, and blinked his way through the night, trying to convince himself that the doctors are wrong. That there is no disease; it's the fever of creation that keeps him awake. In the creeping light of dawn he surrendered his pursuit of sleep and fired up the laptop to spend a little time on his obligations in Darien.

He's got so much on his plate, but there is always something that needs doing here.

My land is as vulnerable to the inexorable slide of entropy as anywhere else. The buildings of New Edinburgh have already succumbed to the damp, garrotted by the vines that bind anything static. My Creator could clear the bush for me at the sweep of his hand, just as he could bestow upon me a castle, a companion or an unending source of food. But, of course, this is not how the divine operate. I am made to understand that I should embrace every challenge that comes my way as a gift. I know I shouldn't question him or his methods, but there is so much that happens in his other life that he can't see, or won't see, or refuses to acknowledge and accept.

Soon enough it breaks through.

If it is indeed Prionic Fatal Insomnia that he has been cursed with, the 'fatal' part of the name is the subject of all his focus. The dim light of the early morning leads his mind to the dark places one would expect. Whether he's facing imminent death or not, he thinks there's a likelihood Brina won't stick around.

With you every step, she has promised, without prompting.

But deep down he knows she doesn't need his nonsense – if he is about to die, she needs to be able to slip from his chains to prepare for a life of her own. Before she gets that freedom she'll have to greet all the relatives and play the grieving widow, and that's just not a role she was put on Earth to fulfil. She is bubbling with life, ravenously hungry for the opportunities it can offer. At this late hour, under the muted glare of the Anglepoise lamp, he sincerely doubts that she will be able to tolerate remaining by his side for months while his powers fade.

§

I want to crawl to him as a thought in the night and say: *You were right, after all. You weren't a hypochondriac.*

§

He spent most of last night researching the disease online. There's a lost irony in the fact that the best hours in which to sleep are wasted searching for information about his insomnia. Even with my existential reliance upon him being awake, I demand that he attempts sleep. There will be plenty of enforced wakefulness in the weeks to come. I need him to rest now if I'm to capitalise on his remaining time.

Prionic Fatal Insomnia – a rogue of a disease. Even the dreaded flux that slithered through New Edinburgh will eventually be seen off with improved hygiene and the advent of antibiotics: my Creator's disorder is different. Only nine cases ever recorded, including him. Does he feel special now?

The oracle of the internet tells him he has something in the region of four months remaining in which he'll be able to write. He'll be exhausted much of the time, but he's already making arrangements to leave his job. This will leave the days free to create, edit and polish. All that's required of me is to keep his attention in the here and now. I can spot the most immediate dangers: he keeps slipping into reveries, lamenting missed opportunities and cringing at moments of failure – these lapses of concentration will be an unacceptable brake on our progress.

Social media causes problems, especially after his fights with Brina. He trawls the net in an attempt to track down every woman he's ever slept with. It's not an ambitious number. He just wants to know where they are, what their lives have brought them. Every single one he's located is married with kids.

There are other women, though, who pose far greater risks to my survival. The coveted creatures with whom he failed to grasp erotic opportunities offered to him – he wonders whether they might not be up for a pity fuck with a dying man? From the trove of photos posted online he has discovered that many of them have grown more attractive with the passing of years.

What is he doing? Why is he stalking women he hasn't seen since they were girls at school?

BEHAVE YOURSELF, I call, *THE WORLD WON'T REMEMBER YOU FOR SOME DESOLATE SYMPATHY FLING.*

Even if he found a woman willing to transgress behind Brina's back, he's not confident he could participate with any satisfaction. He's already saturated in sweat, but there's plenty more to come. The panic attacks haven't taken hold yet – the paranoia and phobias might merely be an extension of the neuroses already familiar to anyone who knows him. And no matter how much time he spends with me – a being of his own creation, stuck in a short lived Scottish colony – his world remains just about rooted in reality. The hallucinations are being kept at bay.

At least this late night poring over the laptop is less sordid and masturbatory than could be the case. I admire that when he isn't shaping my world, he's actually pursuing real information, real knowledge – not watching women perform anatomically impressive feats in sad-looking hotel rooms.

He's not really built for the easy pleasure of porn. He always liked sex, but when he was dealing with porn, or strip clubs, or the rest of the 'industry', he couldn't help indulging the part of his mind that was nourished by novels. All of the women had a back-story, a reason they were doing this rather than something less risky, less exposed. Even after reading academic papers suggesting how well-adjusted the majority of participants in porn were compared to the general population, he still felt it was obvious exploitation. Oddly, in spite of his mild-mannered liberal nature, he's sexist enough to never think of the men. No empathy with them, no concern.

I want to slap him.

Even in my society, those of us who seek enlightenment understand that the sexes are equal in the eyes of the almighty.

§

Praise the mercies that lie upon the earth.

Climbing the rocks above the harbour this morning, in search of good spots for setting up fishing nets, I stumbled across a new source of food: egg-laden nests that lie between the stones.

The eggs are clustered in twos and threes. Dusty pale green and sharply pointed at one end, heavier than they look, but with delicate shells. I collected a handful and considered eating them raw out there on the rocks, but the fear of poisoning cowed my anguished appetite.

I must wait to eat, as my Creator will shortly leave me to feed himself. When he is absent I float in stasis – somewhere between his imagination and the blank page, hidden across the wires and circuit boards of the machine that keeps me alive. Whilst he feeds, I am forgotten. No consideration as he browses the shelves of the fridge.

There are distractions everywhere. Housework is a big one. He doesn't know where to begin with dismantling the daily squalor he accumulates around him. Each evening Brina wearily returns from her work in the city and is immediately confronted with a scene of domestic devastation. He leaves pans on the hob in rings of filth and hurls plastic wrapping into the sink. Brina grits her teeth as she fills the bin bags, knowing she once made a vague promise to support his *art*, but despising his rank laziness.

We did our best to fight against such unequal divisions of labour in the early days of Darien. We harboured dreams of New Scotland growing to be a paradise of equality, regardless of the inherent class differences. Once we had provided our daily bread, the communality of our lives would allow each of us to unlock our own potential. Unfortunately, such noble hopes of civilians were crushed under the glacial pace of progress and the heavy boots of military men. Those trained to carry arms are comfortable only when operating under defined chains of command, arcane structures with little sense to outsiders.

I fell afoul of the martial mode of life, not understanding why I should bow to military authority while engaged in tasks that had nothing to do with sailing or soldiering. I followed their commands when aboard ship or on sentry duty, but when I was one of the few undertaking day-to-day tasks I was unwilling to accept the army overstretching their jurisdiction, and I let them know it.

As the weeks passed the soldiers grew workshy, feeling entitled to put their feet up and bask in our slavery. Many accepted these liberties being taken, supposing the military men would roar into action if we were under threat.

But at the first sight of a ship on the horizon, the bulk of the soldiers busied themselves behind the safety of the tree-line.

We had been deceived.

§

I live in a mirror, reflecting all that my Creator lacks.

He entrusts me to give voice to his failings. The louder I shout the more ground he concedes.

I am the squeaky wheel.

At times he needs cover to hide from his future.

I am his distraction.

Those who crossed the globe with me felt the need to be pious and pitiful creatures under the gaze of their Maker; the unseen hand that can as easily smite them from the Earth as bestow everlasting life. My Creator never asks for effigies or churches, sects or sepulchres. He never needs displays of devotion because he knows the power he yields; what want of a beautiful ceiling or a soaring symphony could be possessed by the being who created everything? These are human things; grubby comforts, grimy pieces of art to make us feel significant – they aren't produced to praise the almighty.

There is no need for supplication, no need to genuflect in his name. He would never ask for that. Religion has nothing to do with the being who paints my world; dogmas and doctrines divorced from creativity. Religion is a creation of man, and anyone who claims otherwise is out to deceive.

I've never known creatures as godless as the kirks who sailed from Scotland. My Creator has made his contempt for their cruelty clear by expunging them from this account. They believed that he spoke to them directly, and felt emboldened to hate, burn and beat in his name. My Creator's judgement was damning – not one minister made it back, he tells me; each struck with flux and hurled overboard, their bodily vessels discarded in the mid-Atlantic.

Since his terminal diagnosis, the almighty has been assessing religious belief. He is angered by those who make moral choices with an eye on everlasting reward or punishment – he's annoyed that they'll never know they were wrong.

When the lights go out, there will be no 'I told you so'.

In his last week of work, he discussed the prohibition of images of the prophet Mohammed with a Muslim friend. He wanted to argue that by passionately pursuing the ban and competing to be more offended than your neighbour, you fall into the idolisation of offence. An immodest worship of victimhood.

His colleague wasn't inclined to engage.

My Creator lacked the words to establish his position – and the intellect. He's used to creating in an environment in which he can edit and polish, and his rambling betrayed the weakness of his debating skills. He confuses being able to remember facts with actual intelligence.

He tries to pass himself off as an intellectual – a flaw that goes all the way back to primary school, before even his first girlfriend found him out. We'll call her Rebecca – she's got her own life and family now, she wouldn't want to be dragged into this. He's been thinking about her a lot lately, particularly about how he embarrassed himself in pursuit of her parents' approval. He tried to keep up but they recognised a half-wit in their house, in ludicrous congress with their daughter. Tolerated to his face and mocked behind his back – he deserved no less. When illness drags him to his lowest, he toys with the idea of contacting her. Meet for one last drink, see if there's any faint affection for the fraud with whom she shared her life for far too long.

§

Now might be the time to return to the start – shed some light on my moment as Lazarus, the moment I learnt about death and accepted my solitary fate:

The decision to stay in Darien followed a final altruistic outburst decrying our leadership. My efforts to enlighten my fellow travellers fell once more upon ears that would not hear.

As a reward I was tied to a tree with ships' rope by the brothers Drummond.

I proclaimed in bound rebellion until muted by exhaustion and my own filth. All around me, plans were made to uproot and turn tail for home. I watched as the collected assets of the Company of Scotland were stowed aboard the ships.

As time crawled past and no one came to my aid, a nagging sense of desperation grew within me.

Addled citizens would sit and stare, and occasionally a bored and aggressive drunk would come forward and box me about the face to entertain the assembled audience.

He's dead, they'd say as they stood over me.

I appealed with my eyes, waiting for the wind-up to end,

for them to untie me and take me on board.

Died days ago, the burliest of the bunch said as he kicked dirt in my face.

I'm not, I replied, I'll keep my tongue from flapping, I can be good.

Definitely dead, said someone at the back.

A jet of phlegm arched over my head and clung flimsily to the bark above.

Food for the worms, announced the burly one as he poked me with a stick.

When he lost interest and left, the rest followed. As they crossed the plain towards the harbour, I resolved to stay in Darien. I had no intention of sharing a ship with their kind.

The moisture of the season did more than spread flux; it gnawed through the ropes that bound me to the tree. The damp set me free, liberated to enjoy my deserted land.

§

Must be vigilant.

My Creator drifted too far from me this afternoon. While travelling on the Underground he caught a sniff of Impulse, the cheap scent Rebecca wore in her adolescence. His mind became awash with memories of inept fumbling and getting half-cut on bottles of wine shared between five. The smell swept past as a girl disembarked the tube. Once the memories dispersed, he felt a sudden anger. He feels incapable of tying it all down – giving voice to his feelings before the end.

§

Lots of time spent on buses now. The hospital visits are essential, but he's no longer behind the wheel – a result of the high cost of hospital parking and the intransigence of his insurer. Best to let someone else do the driving, someone with professional qualifications. They've decided to send him to the National Centre of Excellence. He feels like they expect him to be impressed. Dr Vidmar, his GP, is omnipresent at the appointments that span the country; his own practice must be in disarray. There is a constant cast of figures lurking at the back of rooms, watching, straining to hear, waiting. Waiting is the cornerstone of exploratory medical care. It's also the thread between our lives: I too spend my days waiting, watching my horizon for signs and symptoms of rescue and recovery.

Today's appointment meant the usual armada of personnel. The medicine men and women stayed on the other side of the screens and curtains. A line was scratched in the sand; the people of knowledge on one side, and opposite, my Creator, numbered among the sick animals of the world, tomorrow's carrion.

He watched the doctors deliberate in front of scans projected on a large screen. They took notes but said little within earshot. Everyone involved knows there are no answers. There are some similarities to previous cases, but with something so rare there's never a pattern to discern, no evidence to build upon, no telling trends. Occasionally, an unfamiliar doctor might highlight the fact that important differences to other cases might favour an alternative diagnosis, but these reckless renegades never return for a subsequent visit.

In Darien, we had very little disease beyond the bloody flux. But then, with a plague so efficient at thinning the numbers, no other sicknesses could gain a foothold. We weren't privy to the mechanisms by which illness spread within a population. When armed with that kind of knowledge, even the almighty Creator avails himself of antibacterial gel as he shuffles through hospital corridors.

Test after test. Assessing his blood, his urine, his stool, his bone marrow; his brain activity, his eye movement, his lung capacity, his liver function; his ability to catch a ruler, touch his toes, stand on one leg. They bleed him for every drop of data. Something had changed today, though – there was a graveness in the countenance of the quacks that he hadn't noticed before.

Not so long ago Brina joined him on these tiring trips, but her attendance and support have ebbed away. Her employers were happy to give her time off when it became clear the illness was serious, but they ran out of patience with the hazy diagnosis.

At least, that's the story she's sticking to.

My Creator is relieved in some respects; Brina and Dr Vidmar would gabble away in Slovene, discussing their home towns and local politics; the things they missed, and the things they didn't. Their easy chatter made my Creator feel even more helpless and alone, knowing that he will never have the chance to learn the language to any level of proficiency. Their multilingualism carved a deep line beneath a heavy truth: he has wasted the time he has had.

When left in deliberate ignorance by the doctors, he became annoyed at the nurse who softly teased him for only being able to catch the last millimetres of the ruler that she dropped through his open fist. She was exotically foreign and unreasonably attractive. Had it been his choice he wouldn't have made her that way; her beauty put him on edge. He could smell her perfume and sense her warmth on his neck as she leaned across him to adjust dials and monitors on the wall behind. Hospitals are obliged to be dull, sexless places. He felt aggrieved; humiliated by something that was no one's fault.

§

Before his illness, my Creator kept attempting to learn the Slovene language. It was depressing, watching him struggle with the simplest declension. His teacher, demure and composed in the rest of her life, clenched her teeth with impatience as he stuttered and stumbled through words that would never form.

There's no such difficulty for me. The divine gifts I've been bestowed allow me to converse in any language I wish. My Creator can access instant translations in hundreds of languages with a simple search. No route to fluency, but nearly enough to pass a linguistic Turing test from the confines of his Chinese room. With a combination of keystrokes, I am able to speak without borders:

'Which way is the village?' I may ask a maiden in perfect Sorbian. Or, 'thus were fools ever employed,' I might agree with the chief of the cow-herds in the sublimely accented Tigrinya of the twelfth century.

There are so many tasks that represent insurmountable challenges for him, yet are contemptuously easy for me. All that is required is for him to write something about me and it becomes true.

However, in spite of my powers, he is the agent of their bestowal. I must always be aware that when fatigue gets too much for him, he holds the power to put me to sleep forever. I am obliged to admit these singular abilities. At the flick of his fingers he can drag me from consciousness.

He will torment us, you and I, with this power; like a child who has just discovered the potential of the light-switch. He drags me through the stages of consciousness as a punishment for the throttling wakefulness he must endure. Sunrise to sunset to sunrise to sunset. I am subject to his suffocating love, this abusive parent who carried me in his mind through my gestation, my biography mapped on scraps of paper blue-tacked to the bedroom wall. My likes, my relationships, my struggles, my virtues and vices, all planned before I even began.

And now you're involved. Joint enterprise – no backing out. I'm safe while you're around and I must maintain this triangle. Even when he wilts and lies cold, decomposing, I hope that you and I might be able to carry on together.

I might as well be honest about our relative positions – there's so much more that you can offer me than I can give in return. I'm marooned across oceans and eons. What despicable hubris I show, what ingratitude, what preposterously high ideas so far above my station.

I shan't beg. I'm just happy for us both to agree that I must rely on you parasitically – no – symbiotically. As long as we understand this and are open about it, there's no shame to be borne.

Let all three of us go on together and see what awaits us.

Forgive my inconsistent tone; I'm on edge. I worry I'm being subjected to the first catastrophic bursts of his fatal fatigue. I sense that his dismally inadequate sleeping patterns are taking more of a toll now than before. He could crawl through his life on five hours a night, coping for months at a time, plugging away at the keyboard, flitting over the online papers, Wikipedia and social media. But Brina has been trying to impose some structure since his diagnosis.

Go for a swim, she says as he lies on the floor, groaning at the weight of his task. She knows the value of physical health on the mind: come for a run, we'll just do 5k, she suggests brightly as she slips her toned legs into running tights and begins her stretching. He mumbles his excuses and reawakens the computer.

The problem lies with his erratic patterns. He's been detached for so long, so out of sync with the rest of humanity, that it's impossible for him to tell whether sleep really is harder to acquire or if his brain has learnt to live without it. These are dangerous doubts. His nerves are shot, perhaps another early symptom of the changes taking place. I wish it was within my power to observe the differences objectively – if I could know things outside of his mind I could offer my own diagnosis.

It's so disordered, this world that flows from his mind. As a student he'd shirk his academic responsibilities to spend hours playing computer games, the pile of politics text books an expensive pedestal for his ashtray. He would stay up through the night burning time, pretending to manage a football team. He managed to pull off the illusion that he was a functioning and engaged human being when he wasn't getting drunk or high; but to those closest to him his vampiric existence was a poorly kept secret. They knew all about his other life.

Why should I deride him? My all-powerful and all-knowing Creator. His experiences seem typical of many at that point in their lives, trying to hack a sculpture out of life. My only observation is that he needlessly gave a vast head start to his peers, his competition. He never showed much interest in making money, and I respect that, but think of the novels he could have written in those wasted early years – the years when those truly serious about life were filling their tanks ready to be propelled ever onwards, far out of view.

§

A monumental success – he has stayed up all night with me.

The past hours have mostly been spent scribbling notes, but I feel so alive in my ability to put his shoulder to the wheel. This is a clear victory, even if the resulting fatigue will enfeeble him this morning.

I dare only whisper it, but I feel my power over him growing. He is aware of this; he has no desire to deny the fact. I am to understand that when push comes to shove he is still in control, he won't allow me to grow too strong – he will seek to remind me that I am the vessel of his creativity. He re-asserts that this is a one-way street.

And I am almost convinced.

I suppose I ought to thank the programme of drug therapy – there has been much more clarity since he embarked upon it. The current balance of meds ensures that I can still rise from the sands of Darien and fight for my survival, for now. The polishing I get on the good days means that I can scream across the bay and curse the gods of the ocean instead of watching my skin grow transparent and teeth fall from my jaw. Thanks to the intermittent inner strength he finds, my muscles are strong enough to swim, to hunt, to keep in the chase. I admit to some wear and tear, my skin is reddened by the sun and my teeth are yellow, but they remain robust enough to chew through vines and pull nails from beams.

Aside from sleeplessness, his health has been stable over the past week, and my spirits are heightened. I feel more boisterous. In the first draft I was patchy and inconsistently drawn, but the best thing about an all-powerful Creator is that he can always return to the drawing board.

NEVER STOP, I call to him, and he smiles, attempting empathy for my situation.

He knows that each draft improves upon the last. But he also knows that time and tide are set against any of us ever reaching that moment of ecstatic perfection; so we set sail for the closest course we can, knowing that at some point all of the sand will have fallen from the top chamber to the bottom and there will be no further revision.

In many respects he has a gilt-edged opportunity. His is such a rare experience. Not only is he suffering from an illness that is desperately uncommon, a disorder that fascinates the scientific and medical communities, he also happens to be a writer – someone able to put the experience into words that might bring real emotion to this awful affliction.

But he's too selfish for that, too obsessed with the stories in his head and how faithfully he might be able to carve them onto the page.

And I am with him one hundred per cent.

So much of his time is spent watering arid land, but I believe in every step he is taking here in Darien. I support his devotion to creativity even if it means failing to contribute to the sum of scientific understanding.

Oh, it would be easy for him to dwell and dissect the terror, the pain, the dread, the despair with which his mind is saturated whenever he contemplates the crippling end. He could call up death-row similes, talk of life-sentences, be glib and put on a brave face for the Sunday supplements, but I demand he refuse. To hell with the rest of you and your window on disease. There will be no serialisation for the voyeurs of the dwindling life he must marshal if he is to keep me alive. Don't wait around for the posthumously published misery memoir.

There must be an ending for me, perhaps on a scrap of paper in the bottom of a drawer somewhere. We must wait. He never writes a story whole, from start to finish. He creates a skeleton and over time meat is thrown upon the bones. The muscles grow strong, the brain sharp, the hunger more acute. Even before the illness, his creations would keep him awake at night. He would be burdened by the lives of those he had brought into being and the conflicts they faced.

I will be the last of that illustrious line.

§

He's still not seeking shelter in religion; continuing to claim he's not superstitious to anyone who will listen.

Brina laughs witheringly and asks: What about *Naked Lunch*?

He blushes. This is all the evidence the court needs to convict and she, as his chief prosecutor, can present it at any time.

When he first began reading William Burroughs' *Naked Lunch* in secondary school, his girlfriend of two weeks broke up with him. Later, secure in his relationship with Rebecca he again embarked upon the novel, only for their partnership to immediately fail. When he met Brina, he gave her his copy of the book on the strict condition that she would burn it in an act of sacrificial destruction. A few years later, when they had moved in together, he spotted the book on a shelf during an argument and complained bitterly about its presence. Brina responded with a cutting audit of his character flaws.

At some point during the following months the book disappeared and was never mentioned again.

Is he so superior to shun those who find comfort in religious belief?

§

The ripples of my Creator's life lap upon my shore, nothing I can do about it. Today's message in a bottle tells me that his relationship with Brina has taken a further lurch into the deep tundra of affection. She turns her back on him, and he responds in kind, though only as a response to provocation, trying to show he too can choose to be cruel. She knows him too well, sees through it. She has no place for placid men, no time for those who stand in the shadows. In his moments of lucidity he finds it harder and harder to erect his protective façade. Traps have been laid and he lacks the skill and emotional strength to navigate a safe passage.

In the early days, when there seemed no cost for honesty, he confessed to Brina that he had tried to change his character to fit Rebecca's needs. She brings this up whenever he desperately claims he can reform.

That's not what's happening here, he insists as he jumps up to tidy the kitchen upon her arrival home, anxious that his behaviour isn't seen as door-mattery. The more he fakes a front of strength, the crueller Brina becomes.

She sighs dramatically, slinging sarcastic laughter at him when he opens the dishwasher and realises it's been waiting all day to be emptied.

You're going to be tidy for your last two months, are you? Best later than never, she sneers.

The phrase is '*better late* than never,' he corrects her, sensing a tiny win that is no victory whatsoever. She shakes her head and leaves without a further word.

She chips away at him when he's at his weakest, so he clings to the moments when wine has warmed her affections. Late on Saturday night she whispers to him with sour breath:

I will miss you terribly. He clutches those words close and dreams that they are fixed for a moment.

My Creator tries to ignore the fact that the odds are against him. They all grow tired of him in the end. How does he account for that? They are quick to fall in love, but once they get to know him, they make their excuses and leave.

STOP DWELLING ON THIS.

Think of me.

In some ways, his conjugal failure benefits me. As Brina sits watching the television with the face of thunder she drags home most nights, he seeks refuge in the keys of his laptop, spending his time in Darien.

Today I'm on a hiding to nothing. Whenever he hears my calls his mind sinks to the simmering resentment he feels towards Brina. He's certain all of the men at her work are already experts on the subject of their relationship, and her weakening faith in it. Her use of social media has become far more furtive; as soon as he lifts his head he can see her closing apps. When they watch films together she engages in a constant exchange of messages with a third party.

He is grindingly suspicious that everyone else knows more than he does.

He is being frozen out – queasy at the prospect of feeling the absolute loss of intimacy that arrives with the collapse of a relationship. He remembers it. Like a switch, one day a woman is happy to dress in his company, the very next he is banished from the room.

He missed something somewhere.

When his mind is in this place I know I must bide my time and wait for tomorrow.

§

My Creator has only himself to blame for the times he was single. Long barren spells when his aloneness didn't bother him until he was part of a pair again; then, as if a great epiphany, he would suddenly realise he'd been sickeningly lonely for as long as he could remember. He had convinced himself that the freedom of not having to consider someone else's wants and needs was adequate compensation, but what had he done with that freedom? Drink heavily, sleep all day, and hop between jobs being torn by barbs of unrequited desire. What a waste. When given all that time to write he'd choose instead to go on the prowl until the sun rose, then sleep until mid-afternoon, shower, eat and head back out. Now, in the dimming embers, he feels the need to chastise himself and share his regret with others, in the hope that he might be a warning to them.

I'm not convinced he really means it; he's too fond of wallowing.

Brina has clearly grown tired of his slump towards death. She won't have to hang on for too long – a year would probably suffice for the sake of appearances. Then she can throw herself into a new life. She'll play the bereaved survivor who endured something truly and terribly exceptional; there will be drugs and beds and trips and travel if that's what she desires. She can indulge any whim to tell anyone to fuck off, and for months she'll get away with it. Every occurrence of erratic behaviour will be excused and indulged. Having spent the prime years of her life with a writer, someone only prepared to share half of himself – the other half spent secluded in his own head – she can look forward to less selfish lovers, to her own story being of sole importance.

She's nearly off the hook.

§

When three o'clock arrives on a weekday afternoon, he listens to the children leaving the school down the road and remembers the daily milestone that moment represented throughout his childhood. He left school half his life ago. It's perverse to retain such an attachment to former routines, but this is how he divides his life up. A few years ago, he worked out the exact moment he had lived for longer since school than he had spent there. He marked the occasion with a night in the pub.

I wasn't on the scene then, but if I had been, I'd have made my feelings known.

NONE OF YOUR PEERS REMEMBER THESE DATES.

He's the only one clinging on.

It's not that he can't move forward, just that he can't escape this obsession with anniversaries. When he was a smoker he obsessed about how close he was to having spent more of his life as a smoker than not. How many cigarettes had he smoked? Laid end-to-end, how far would they reach?

Perhaps I should go easy on a dying man. We all need to retain some connection to the days that have passed.

The three o'clock wash of infant voices is a church-bell tolling on the edge of my Creator's consciousness. In his drive towards isolation, he no longer knows the day of the week. He can remember a gig he played at the Point in Oxford when he was seventeen, down to the songs in the set, but he isn't sure if today is Tuesday or Thursday. I'm surprised he surrenders this knowledge, given the time he spends reflecting on the rootlessness of his heavy-drinking phase (his term). He agonised over how unhitched he had become from normal society. An endless cycle of piss-up followed by hangover, followed by piss-up that wrenched him out of daily life.

Impending disaster would always materialise with an unforeseen obligation in the morning hours. He would be summoned to the bank or invited to a job interview and a suffocating panic would tighten around him as he fretted over how he might get his shit together for nine o'clock in the morning. How could such a reasonable demand derail him?

Somewhere along the line he learnt how to look after himself, just in time for his brain to start disintegrating.

§

A morning spent online, reading academic articles on climate change and the potential effects of mass-migration. My Creator is becoming preoccupied with the 'great issues of the day': the issues that could further the cause of humanity, leave a legacy. He deceives himself that he might achieve something more than this historical novel. I tell him not to lose focus – the most important thing he can do is share with the world the hope, failure and desperation of those in history who tried to build a better life on the other side of the planet.

His desire to finish my story waxes and wanes. He assails the peaks and troughs as they come. Often he is gripped by a potent and productive fever. I am subject to all of his attention, all of his creative endeavour, and I thrive on my little patch of land. But there are other times when he hides away, curled in a corner leafing through old photo albums. From those fading images I have come to understand a truth that has thus far escaped me: while his presence maintains my survival, he has no one on whom to lean, no one whose ongoing attention nourishes and protects him. He is the end of the line, the alpha and omega. He has only prions, unthinking strands of protein, strings of senseless nothing that will soon call time on his life.

That's true cruelty. For all the rage I direct at him for the storms, the lack of food and the fading hope, at least I can attempt to reason with him. The unwelcome director of my Creator's own story is composed of nothing more than rogue bundles of misfolded amino acids. There's no reasoning to be done: it's not even bacteria. Nothing living, no contribution to life, just dumb ruination.

There may be a cure one day, but there's nothing in the pipeline yet. In a few months, after he has left me for the confines of a hospital bed, there will be no chance of a pioneering surgeon sweeping in to deliver him from death. For all the medical attention, the world is not a millimetre closer to fixing him than it was before he was diagnosed.

He has embraced this fact. It's why I'm here, and it's why he spends so much time poring over his past, reanimating those who have passed through his life.

Even so, it's a near impossible task to really come to terms with what's in store; could anyone really do it in good faith?

Perhaps my story will sufficiently reflect the state of his psyche. I can't discount that possibility. My life on Darien may help to illustrate how it feels to stare down the barrel of this particular gun. But let us not forget that an editor will get hold of this, first readers, the publisher. Outsiders will take turns to stick an oar in. This text may have looked very different in his last completed draft.

Who will ever be able to say?

Once my Creator is out of the picture, plenty of people will bring their own agendas and expectations to bear upon his creation. Some will regard his words with affection, some with suspicion and others with disappointment. Whatever happens, I don't want anyone to doubt for a moment that someone lived within these pages. Someone who strived for their reach to exceed their grasp.

§

The early hours of the morning mark the most precious time I spend in the mind of my Creator. Here he writhes like a maggot, consuming the emotional decay of his private past, privy only to me. Triggers are everywhere: music brings on the strongest memories, especially when aided by alcohol. He shouldn't feel any shame. Everyone has murk in their past, but his impending mortality means he delights in plumbing his own depths. He's so un-godlike when he gives free reign to his own eroticism – you should see the material that was cut. Unnecessary pornography that did nothing to further my story.

Morally at least, the light is already fading.

§

My Creator's growing incoherence is starting to publicly embarrass him, and he's pained that he won't survive long enough to get comfortable with the changes that Prionic Fatal Insomnia has brought to his life. There'll be no opportunity to learn to live with his disorder.

He's just returned from the convenience store on the corner, seething with indignation at the rudeness of the shopkeeper. My Creator's crime? He dared to dither. With his brain AWOL at a crucial moment, the ignorant merchant barked at him: choose or fuck off (to paraphrase). He fumed his way homewards, determined to record his thoughts and summon an appropriate response, but he was met by this page. I dragged him back into my world.

In his infinite wisdom, he has long felt that the majority of people who claim to 'not suffer fools gladly' are themselves dull idiots. This comes despite his own past experience of Rebecca and her mother. Both women were far from fools; indeed, they were intelligent to the point of intimidating him. His idiocy brought barely disguised impatience to their words and actions, but he was too stupid to realise until it was too late. Cockily unaware of his intellectual limitations whilst sitting at their dinner table, he sailed through the whole affair in a state of blissful ignorance. Constantly trying to keep up, to hold his corner, to endear himself to them. But every effortful tale, every poorly judged bon-mot, every ill-thought-out opinion was received with polite smiles and swift changes of subject.

He was out of his depth and is mortified to realise it only now, so far after the original offence. He thought they were his people. He felt he belonged. It's clear now that he must have looked preposterous, trying to better himself, developing opinions on the hoof, mispronouncing words he didn't know how to use. They pitied him. He was completely unaware, blinded by over-confidence brewed from a blend of youthful ignorance and the intoxication of being in love for the first time. He was no match for the all-consuming devotion that accompanied his teenage desire. But Rebecca was never playing for real. At university she discovered a world of people who understood the carefully chosen words that came from their own mouths; people possessed of a slick private-school confidence, unselfconscious about advertising their own qualities and damning those who didn't fit.

Rebecca found a tribe and she wanted in.

Even now, listening to Tricky's 'Maxinquaye' and immersed in memories of those days, he can't help but cringe when confronted with what an idiot they must have made of him.

Hell is round the corner.

NO USE LOOKING BACK ALL THE TIME.

At some point it all has to stop.

I just need some fucking sleep.

§

To succeed, I must goad my Creator when his guard is down.

I catch him desperately trying to record everything before it's too late. Crawling into his ear I whisper to him of the genuine greats, those who had far more courage and skill than he will ever muster, even with the monolithic motivation of death rising in the distance. He will never have the balls to face the senselessness of the world as they did, or to truly explore his emotions under the public gaze. My monologue takes him to Gogol, shivering over a brazier heated by religious fervour and the glowing pages of his manuscript. He destroyed his creation. Posterity was no reward for him, no bait. He had more focus, more composure; with the purest intent he burnt his book and then starved to death.

When my Creator began writing, he was propelled by a simple dream of being able to take his book down from the shelf or, less modestly, spying the spine among the rows in a bookshop. As he grew older his arrogance matured. He thought that with hard work, he might manage to fool the world that he emerged in some moment of singularity, a writer with no antecedents, a Kafka for his own time. Even if he had been born with the requisite talent it was a futile fantasy. He would have run into British anti-intellectualism, there would never be the sales numbers to make such high ideas successful. A new Kafka wouldn't make sense – he would be denounced as elitist; a purveyor of highfalutin ideas way above the station of anyone worthy of society's esteem.

My Creator missed his moment – that's what he tells himself as he gazes at his reflection on the window pane. With death closing in, I'm inclined to give him that. Who knows? Given more time maybe he could have become someone.

The End overshadows everything; the harder he works to engage with the external, the more he sinks into his inner world.

§

Robinson Crusoe: it's an obvious comparison to make but I suffer by it. Crusoe was an industrious soul with an inventive mind, who no doubt relished being marooned. His inventiveness was the trait of someone who found themselves in surroundings favourable to their temperament; he didn't need to cling to survival with his last ounce of strength.

I am the victim of callous abandonment.

Crusoe could be complacent, safe in the knowledge that he would adapt and innovate to survive.

For me, there is always the possibility that time might run out on my Creator, and I will be trapped. If that comes to pass, I will have to rely on the benevolence of others to ensure that I find resolution.

I shall say kind words to them now, those eminent gatekeepers, those paragons of imagination, in the hope that some kindly soul amongst them has arranged for a ship to be sent on its way.

Sometimes I must question how I spend my days, how I

spend my Creator's time. I worry I've no right to pray for my ship of salvation when he is facing the end of his life. He is soon to endure the descent from the glory of being someone to being merely something – a body, disposed of according to local laws. While he faces his destruction, I lie here, morosely speculating on whether I will ever return to Scotland.

Why does my ego obsess over such things? I need to ensure my survival, not fiddle while Rome malevolently glows. I must take control, make my own luck, conjure some food from somewhere – get down to learning how lobster traps work.

Are jellyfish edible? I'd need to work out how to neutralise the venom – I've no way of dealing with a self-poisoning. My ignorance speaks volumes: Defoe ensured that Crusoe was capable, strong of mind, built to survive. He was able to handle the rigours of loneliness and despair; he didn't doubt himself.

I survive on a diet of doubt, hopelessness and creeping contempt for the blockage at the centre of my universe. In this moment, I am almost glad he's dying. We will all find freedom when he is gone.

§

A crushing sense of futility follows each Slovene lesson.

My Creator probably has a month and a half of useful brain function left and still he insists on trying to learn a language he has always found impenetrable. This commitment comes from guilt; guilt that he didn't make enough effort when it might have mattered, back when he had a future. With a little more talent or a lot more application he might have equipped himself to speak to Brina's parents in their own language. They would have been impressed;

far more so than with the cack-mouthed crushing of their Slavic tongue that he has managed. The first time he stumbled through, 'I think Slovene is a very difficult language because I am stupid,' they laughed. The twentieth time it was just sad.

I have to accept that my Creator has such failings.

Znam slovensko, menim, da je zelo lahek jezik – how hard can it be? And he's the father of the universe. That's the difference between us, I guess. He scrutinises me from his position of corporeal presence and flimsy reality. In these cases, it occurs that I might be the one with real power. The writer will be a flawed and fallible beast, but the written; well, the written can be anything or anyone. There is no limit to where or when I could come from or go to. I can be the tiniest elemental particle or encompass everything. I can speak every language, walk on water, or die for an eternity and be reborn. I can be my Creator, I can be you, I can be all. Maybe I don't have the privilege of your narrow sense of existence, but I'm as real as anything else you'll find in a book.

I have an axe to grind today – that's coming through. It's clear that in order to communicate with a reader, I must fight through the filter of my Creator. He is the gatekeeper and I am condemned to be the man from the country who asks to be admitted. He shakes his head as I approach the gate. I ask him to admit me at every idle moment.

It is possible, he tells me this much.

But if he had real power, if he was able to give me a physical body with some mass beyond the page, oh then I would shine. I would barge past the first gatekeeper and deal with the others as they came. That's how those born of privilege crush the rest of us – they are raised being told the gatekeeper is always subordinate to them. An unskilled manual worker; the face of an authority they can choose to ignore. They don't wait to be granted admission.

Be brave.

These options aren't open to me.

I am obliged to work with my Creator. If I have good fortune, then he will hold the door open and push me through, bewildered, blinking into the light. I am never permitted to hide in the darkness. I'm chained to him, as he is to me. We are each the rock the other must spend every day relentlessly rolling uphill, only for it roll back down over night. As the sweats and panic attacks become a more regular feature of his lucid life, we shall both be forced to retire from the public sphere, able to roll our respective rocks in peace.

At these moments it dawns on me that although we have shared so much of this tale with you, the final parts must occur off-screen. The terminus of my Creator's life will arrive locked in his flickering mind, far from the page. He is unlikely to experience a single sensation of its passing.

RESCUE ME BEFORE THE END.

My fate is subject to divine decree. Permit me to pray for a moment.

But the words never come to mind
at moments like these.

Put me on board a ship in the midst of a storm and I'm as loquacious as I am pious, but when given a quiet moment the silence rings in my skull. It's telling that the words flow uncontrollably when I choose to curse my Creator – for he is cracked and fragile amongst all that is sublime in the universe. If the good book tells me to owe creation to his perfect and infinite wisdom, then he must take ownership of all that is desolate and festering as well.

It cannot be forgotten that this universe of unending possibility is also home to both his illness and my abandonment. Where is the sublime in our lives? Where's the compassion, the wisdom, the sense?

What a slender anti-prayer.

I should cut my losses before I displease him. These debates are for another time.

If I am prepared to work with him, we can creep towards those titanic truths that rule over life and bring some hint of them to the page. There must be some truths it is within our limited talents to tell. My life has been lived in a very different environment to yours. With a little less self-awareness I may have been more protected, but I don't wish to live in bad faith. I have the courage to admit that I know almost nothing, but I have seen things, I carry memories. I have witnessed so many dead; I have been surrounded by life grown cheap. These are truths. The cosseted Western hemisphere of your time shelters you from such things. Modern medicine and the welfare state prevent close proximity to the bodies of the dead. And yet here, here I had to share my bunk with the bloated corpse of Arthur Stevens while we waited to make landfall. I've seen boys run through with blades for slipping a careless word at the gambling table. I've seen mothers and daughters debased by the broiling desire of the bestial mob. Those who choose to travel across the world in search of a better life are obeying the ape part of their brain – this is how our species spread across the entire planet.

§

We have an uneasy relationship with these truths. It is both a curse and a blessing that my Creator writes from the perspective of the early twenty-first century. The differences between our times often catch me unawares.

In my time, for example, we have no doubt about the identity of Shakespeare.

My Creator came late to an appreciation of Bill. Alienated, like most of his peers, by the fossilised deference attached to the teaching of Shakespeare's work. It took the passion and perseverance of a Chipping Norton School English teacher to reveal *Hamlet* in all its brilliance. His eyes were opened. Hamlet was a man of words, not actions, and this resonated with my Creator in his teenage years.

The tragedy of Hamlet, his impotence of indecision – my Creator understood that Shakespeare had something vital to say. Shit or get off the pot, the bard bellowed across the centuries. When you get the chance, stand up and take your best shot.

But what is the senseless need for some of your contemporaries to turn Shakespeare into an upper-class conspiracy? I am privileged that my story resides in these pages in spite of my humble origins. The near entirety of British history is the recorded life of monarchs and the aristocracy. This is offensive enough, but for those charlatans to attempt to claim Shakespeare for the upper classes; this betrays a grave sickness.

It is entirely plausible that a lad from Stratford-upon-Avon could have created Shakespeare's oeuvre.

There are enough errors in his work to know he was a man of imagination who cared little for facts. Those who conspire to steal him from the people are those in thrall to the establishment, fattened on a fascination with wealth and power. They sow doubt with bogus theories and seek to muddy previously clear waters.

It does a disservice to the truth.

> *What is truth? Said jesting Pilate,*
> *and would not stay for an answer.*

Readers are always so obsessed with the truth – narrative truth – the sincere verisimilitude of literature. That battle was lost long ago. So much art is dedicated to the myths descended from Jesus, or Mary, or Judas when shame is to be evoked, but the real truth is that we are all descended from Pilate. His Gospel is carved across the face of the modern world: I see it in the sea glass and hear it swirling in conch-shells. It is told through the routine and bureaucracy to which you subject yourselves.

My Creator is no different to anybody else. He wants to believe that there is some truth in literature that can't be reached through other routes. But in his cowardice he took the easier route throughout his younger years; he gave his sweat to the unthinking life of the worker-consumer.

When there are bills to pay, literature makes no ripples in the world according to Pilate's gospel.

§

I'm awake, but in a bad way.

The sun has dropped in the sky, but my eyes are swollen, my skin is tight and I can feel the heat radiating from me. I have erred greatly.

The fool on the shore.

I have recklessly slept under the furnace glow of the Darien sun, with no shelter. As I move my arms and legs, the skin covering the junctions of my joints stabs me with pain. A neuro-chastisement for making such a fundamental error.

My head throbs, crushed in the vice of dehydration.

My tongue is split to the top of my throat. A slash of complaint at being cooked alive.

Golden fucking rule – don't let the elements in.

Jesus, if it hurts this much now, I can just imagine the agony I've got waiting for me over the coming hours.

§

Sunstroke hauls me in and out of fevered slumber. The stuttering dreams drag me back to his memories, always back to *his* fucking memories. He spends so much time embedded in scenes from his past. Just now: a soft spring evening in the house on Lake Street, naked next to Rebecca, listening to Wire, feeling his body brushed by the early evening breeze that hushed through the window.

Entirely at peace.

I awake sweating, in pain, and scratch the word 'Legacy' in the clay. This is how I convince him to leave those soothing memories. He forces himself to write about me. He is growing to hate me as he sees the time he has left evaporating.

CHANGE THE RECORD.

I lose consciousness again as his mind slides back to running naked through a corridor in Hertford College searching for toilet roll to erase the evidence of early experimentations with womankind. There as an interloper, smuggled in on a summer's evening.

These reels of memory are important tools to him. I understand that they provide imaginative capital with which to create events in my world, but in my hyperthermic state I must apply a cold compress to his headspace and keep the recollections to a minimum.

§

The healing process has raised weeping blisters on my cheeks. I wake with my face stuck to the cloth I sleep upon and have to tear myself free from the yellowing crust.

Intense itching occupies our evenings. The house is quiet tonight. Brina decamps to stay with a male colleague on a semi-regular basis. My Creator and I are both too restless in the hours of darkness, and she needs to maintain more orthodox patterns.

My Creator protested when she announced her plan, but Brina is stubborn and he concedes that she might have a good reason to seek sanctuary elsewhere.

He is sceptical that she is managing to get more sleep in her temporary bed.

§

I peel a vast sheet of spent skin from my back and shoulders. A diaphanous skein of vellum parchment on which to write someone else's story.

So many stories. My Creator worries the novel is nearly broken. Destroyed by neglect, by a malign devotion that suffocated it from an art form into a heritage industry. The end of the novel is a trope that can be exhumed ad-infinitum. Inhabiting the pre-Crusoe world, I look forward to all the novels that are to come, the great adventures and experiments that have long since become passé for you. In your shoes I might wring my hands about the end of ideas; the concept that there can be no more originality, sacrificed to the wheezing feedback loop of remakes and re-imaginings. Your cultural legacy will be reboots and ironic sequels.

How does it feel?

The post-ness of culture; post-ideas, post-creation, post-hype. Don't believe it for a second.

OPEN YOUR EYES.

§

My Creator has just wasted a couple of hours scrolling through his wish list at a ubiquitous online retailer. He craves books he'll never read. He pauses to look around at the unread piles he already owns.

Worse still, he's added twenty books to the list since his diagnosis. I try to tell him that when he is confined to his hospital bed there won't be much reading happening.

Dribbling/incontinence/incomprehension: yes

Reading: not so much.

I let him break to watch television from time to time, but he understands that any activity that doesn't relate directly to me will be accompanied by my constant nagging.

He is too terrified to ignore the ideas that I whisper into his mind. No chance he'd risk not getting them down. It's the same tactic I use at two in the morning when he lies next to Brina, blinking into the darkness. I speak over his consciousness, drifting in from the background buzz, and send him grasping for the notebook he keeps at his bedside.

Invariably, Brina wakes straight away.

Go to the living room, she moans, theatrically flailing her arm at him. The great Creator shrinks and scampers off to the solitude of the cold living room. There he kneels, shivering, writing longhand as fast as he can, racing the words through his brain before they dissipate uselessly through his skull and out into the troposphere.

He's being dramatic – it's no real inconvenience. Everybody suffers moments of intrusive inspiration. They're like the ships that trouble my sleep as they skirt the horizon.

Each night I lie down to rest, knowing that I must be ready to fight at the sound of a footstep. I sleep lightly, ready to wake at the slightest rustle.

As if I don't have enough to contend with.

Look at my feet, smeared with grime from shuffling across the sand. I don't have the energy to lift them. This isn't even really sand; more a sludge of chewed up plant matter, crushed rock and clay. Vegetation grows right to the shoreline, so the beach I speak of needs to be cleared through hard labour and constant maintenance. The wider neighbourhood is dense undergrowth, unyielding lattices of knotted wood, occasionally hooded in a damp fog. Rapid transit is strictly prohibited.

I remember vague geographical details from the delicate brushwork I committed to the colony's charts, but as someone versed in the use of the theodolite and the sextant, landscape learned late in life does not lodge reliably in my mind's eye without the prompt of a map. The jungle is so tangled and the hills so tightly folded that I see little value in solo exploration. For anything essential I know I could contact the Kuna, but by and large I sit tight in my little spot and remain undisturbed.

Even that term – *undisturbed* – is a farce. Nothing is ever still in this sultry pit, though the bats are the only beings that move with anything approaching vigour. They explode into the sky as dusk falls. There must be a cave. I've often thought about trying to find the location, but always talk myself out of it. I'd just end up covered in guano and no doubt miss the one friendly ship that passes by while trying to locate the roost.

If such a ship will ever come.

When comfortable and confident, I tell myself that my destiny is in safe hands. I'm strong when I've got some fight in me. Faith burns without fuel and my faith burns as brightly today as any other.

In contrast, my Creator is feeling low. While he grapples to accept his future, he is dispirited by the deafening ticks of the clock counting out the hours he has left. The emptying well of time doesn't motivate him into action as much as he thought it would when the diagnosis was handed down.

His mother called earlier.

She's trying to convince him to write a list of all the things he'd like to do. He snarled and accused her of being maudlin. It might surprise you, but I have no problem with him ticking off a few last wishes, as long as he takes a notebook. It's nice to get out of the house. There are all kinds of connections he makes during unguarded moments when not wracking his brain in front of the laptop. He's least nimble when trying to *THINK*, trying to *CREATE*.

I can't claim to understand how the unconscious works. All I know is that it provides cover, allowing me to slip into his mind to nag and niggle and ensure my ongoing survival. I just wish I could wander around at will and find out what he plans for my future. Perhaps he hasn't decided yet – but I know there have been several drafts. No Creator works entirely on the hoof; although some seem to conceive their worlds before sitting back to see where it takes them.

Absentee landlords – there should be a plan for everything.

If one is arrogant enough to take on the creation of the universe and giving life to another, then they should at least possess a whiteboard covered in notes, diagrams and timelines with which to be guided. Otherwise, it's neglect-ful, a dereliction of what an omnipotent Creator owes to their work.

To my credit, I am a creation who won't go quietly. I cannot afford to waste a single wind, current or opportunity to get home. I will not squander the life I have already lived on scraps of paper and flipchart sheets. Not to get too Tristram Shandy, but my own conception was a furtive squirt of ink into a Moleskine notebook deep in the working day. Until I flickered into view, my Creator had his mind on an entirely different universe – I tempted him into promiscuity.

But now I am the end of the line.

No one will muscle in on my patch.

My Creator won't be around much longer and I have the glorious knowledge that no plans have been hatched for the next universe. There will be no new additions to the multiverse of characters, plots and styles over which he previously obsessed and studied. I am the end of his road and I get his entire creative life to myself.

Now, *GET ME OUT OF HERE.*

§

I didn't make much progress today. I'd intended to fix the roof of my dwelling, but my Creator's mind is consumed by an almighty row with Brina. He made the mistake of mentioning an email he received from a television producer, discussing the possibility of making a documentary about his illness.

Brina broached the subject over last night's cottage pie.

I think you should do it, she announced. He told her they wouldn't pay him anything for it. That's not the point, she replied. It would give the illness exposure, help others come to terms with it, let them know not to worry.

My Creator bristled: if there are others, they definitely need to fucking worry.

He believes that he's keeping drama out of his life by

refusing to allow his final months to become a televised freak show.

That phrase, 'freak show', has become a dog whistle term between them. It's too close to the bone, too raw. He can handle the international road show of doctors – it's the longest of long shots, but their attentions might spring him from his trap – but the ragtag pilgrimage of distant family friends and long lost ex-colleagues is already too much without his plight being beamed into the nation's living rooms. Just think of the mawkish moths that would be drawn to his glowing death following that kind of publicity. He suspects that some people are already visiting him in the hope that there will be cameras – this trickle would swell to a tsunami if he agreed to the nationwide broadcast.

Brina insists it might lead to other things, opportunities that will provide payment, secure revenue streams: money that could help him with end of life care, cash that could help her when the inevitable happens. This last part riles him. Recently she's been spending most nights at her colleague's. He wonders why she's suddenly so concerned that there might be some money on the table.

How could he allow cameras in to witness this unedifying unravelling?

After dinner he was too vocal in his suspicions about Brina's intentions.

She claimed she'd lived with him as a wife, asked whether she didn't deserve the same rights as if they'd been married?

In no mood to discuss the political implications of co-habitation, my Creator responded that if she really felt that way, she wouldn't have moved in with someone else and left him to fend for himself.

There can't be too much of this, my story is too important. How their tale will end seems obvious.

I have to admit confusion at the complexity of their domestic situation. In Darien, and back in Scotland, we didn't change our arrangements as fluidly as is acceptable in my Creator's epoch. All of his peers seemed to embark upon a series of casual relationships before settling down; this would have been scandalous in New Edinburgh.

My civilisation is big on scandal. When I erred in my role as a gaoler, my small swathe of society revelled in its pursuit of clamouring judgement. There was no limit to my denunciation, even though I was a frontline public servant, a correctional officer in a world where the ultimate corrective was a noose. I was imperfect, had a solitary stumble, made a single mistake. This alone was enough to convict me in the court of public opinion, a far more fearsome punishment than the fine and loss of employment imposed by the magistrate.

As a man of humble but acceptable standing I hoped, indeed, expected, that I might be afforded the benefit of the doubt. But there's no such thing in small communities. Such populations regulate themselves through informal punishments and the silent, but ever-present, threat of ostracism. For this check and balance to work most effectively, there must be periodic purges of personnel.

Even if it's once every couple of generations, the folk memory must retain the fear.

The convicted woman in my charge at least had the luxury of having been tried by her peers in accordance with legal process; in my informal condemnation by the community I wasn't invited to enlist a solicitor, have access to court records or recourse to a higher authority. In the savage justice of the social sphere there is no higher court than the outraged neighbourhood – to which no appeals may be lodged.

My Creator worries that this is just as true of the justice of social media. If he allows the documentary to be made, it won't just be acquaintances that he'll have to contend with, it'll be rubber-necking strangers and trouble-makers taking to their keyboards to humiliate and castigate him. 'Freak show' wouldn't begin to describe the scorn and accusation that would be hurled at him from the dark recesses of cyberspace.

§

Brina is bristling with anger and my Creator is trying to ignore the fact.

She has tolerated being kept at a distance during their time together. He has taken this for granted, usually stuck in his own mind, making up stories; like a fucking child.

Today they further discussed what will happen when he's gone. It brought them closer for a while, until he broke the spell. He caught a snatch of song seeping through the window and his shutters dropped as he tried to place it.

St Ives, he mumbled, we listened to it in St Ives.

We've never been, Brina replied as she stroked his cheek.

Not you – Rebecca, he snapped thoughtlessly back.

She pushed him away and went to the kitchen.

She doesn't have to put up with this shit. Not with everything else he's dragging her through.

He went into the garden to write and found me sitting waist deep in the sea.

Over the past few days I've noticed dense shoals of fish orbiting the shallows off the sandbank. With the aid of two lengths of wood, I reckon on being able to marshal the fish onto the submerged plateau.

Nudge the right plank.

Nudge the left plank.

Patience is a skill I have developed in the pursuit of food.

Right plank.

Left plank.

A couple of sharp ones slip away but hundreds remain.

Left plank.

Right plank.

Drag my arse across the seabed an inch or two and restart the process.

Right plank.

Left plank.

Let a little water out.

Let the surface settle.

Left plank.

Right plank.

I sense fortune on my side, shepherding these fish to their unwitting demise.

Fish-herd?

Right plank.

Left plank.

The lengths of wood allow me to cover several square yards of seabed.

I'm moving as slowly as possible, pausing on occasion to pack sand behind the boards for security.

Left plank.

Right plank.

The only flaw in my dam is the small breach where the planks join between my legs. This allows the enclosed water to seep away, keeping the surface still and absorbing the shock of my less placid movements.

I shiver from adrenaline and the breeze that pricks through my saline-sopped clothes.

I look down at the fish.

The fish look back at me.

We watch and wait.

Left.

Right.

Inch by inch towards the shallows, closer to my stomach. My slow, fluent actions now cease to disturb the seabed.

Right.

Left.

In two hours I have brewed a thick soup of slithering fish.

Edge the planks across, close the breach.

Holding the wooden boards like this, I create a pool that will feed me for weeks – provided I strengthen it against the tides.

This is a challenge to ponder upon.

After concentrating so hard for so long, I'm happy to sit and watch my prize while the sea laps at my ribs. Resting, I feel a deep fatigue. The fish grow bold in this tranquillity, the braver ones swim against my hands, testing their boundaries.

A white flash and a splash.

I watch the bird loop into the treeline with a jack-knifing fish in its claws.

The sudden disturbance sends the rest of the fish barrelling against the join in the planks. They slap and thud around my waist as they tumble to freedom. I grab at the stragglers, but by removing the pressure from the planks my dam collapses and in no time I am left with nothing but a bloom of gritty water.

I slip backwards into the brackish bay and stare at the sky while the waves roll over me.

Rarely have I felt so low since arriving in Darien.

As the surf shuffles me from side-to-side, I am ready for my Creator to decide he is done with me. My hope ebbs away on the surface of the Caribbean.

But I have survived up to this point, and I have the ear of my Creator.

That is the key.

The almighty Creator is chronicling my struggle; a struggle he shares. After the millennia it is his turn to bear witness. I lavish praise upon him and his wisdom. I make hasty promises to build an ark, so long as I am permitted to squeeze in among the two-by-two. I beg him to wash away the sins of the world. Better still, give me a woman and the chance to create a son. I would take my child to the Creator's altar in a heartbeat to show I mean business.

> *Offer him there for a burnt offering*
> *upon one of the mountains.*

I walk from the water, reinvigorated in spite of the day's futile labours.

§

In the first draft, my Creator was intensely devoted to verisimilitude. He was committed to subduing our disbelief.

No longer. Tiredness inevitably won out. With each polishing, hiding the lies becomes more exhausting, more impossible, more pointless.

In any case, there was never any need for him to fret over the deception.

There was help at hand.

I don't know how open I can be about the role of the editor. My Creator is the first such gatekeeper, and might resist me revealing too much.

We shall see.

Since his earliest skirmishes with each draft of the manuscript, many other hands have been laid upon me. This interference has freed me from fear about finding the right words: I can suck lousy utterances back into my mouth and replace them with something better – never perfect, but better. I shall never be pained by staircase wit, plagued by a cutting response that only reveals itself to my mind once the moment has passed.

L'esprit de l'escalier

Everyone's an editor, a universal truth that has come late to my Creator. He thought it was a task that only concerned artists, but as he trawls through his memories, past hopes and frustrations, conversations, people come and gone, he realises editing is intimately allied with memory. He took Brina to the Pompidou Centre, having passionately described the building and its contents gleaned from memories laid down during a school trip.

Pete climbed down the front
of the hotel to buy fags one night.

He was stunned by how little reality corresponded to his recall. Everything was out: the proportions of the square, the surrounding streets, the height of the building, the size and shape of the galleries. The margin by which his memory was wrong profoundly shocked him. He wanted to flee from the scene. The experience forced him to distrust his recollection, he realised that in order to thrive he must embrace an approach that can accommodate life as it is actually encountered. Knowing he could never dip his toe in the same river twice, he aimed to look only forward.

An admirable ambition, but we're all stuck with our point of view, the venerable Creator as much as myself. It's healthy to desire to look forward, to ensure that we don't spiral into a permanent state of paralysing reflection, struck dumb by the weight of our memories. But there are no concrete images in the futures we paint for ourselves, none of the easy comfort that memory provides. We can cling to ephemeral hopes, but what value do they have compared to the knowledge entwined within memories? Perhaps a ship will come, perhaps it won't; maybe they will find a cure, maybe they won't. My Creator and I fuse together through the mutual hopelessness that comes from being blind to what the future holds.

I understand now that this is why he won't reveal my destiny to me – he needs have a partner in ignorance.

He needs something to pull him onwards, to get him on his feet each day.

§

Brina left.

He didn't come here to write; not for a long time.

He marks her departure with long spells spent thinking about his youth.

What else?

He looks across at the trees in the small park out back and lets his memory slip over his school days like a silk sheet. Not unquestionably the best days of his life – it would be unfortunate to claim that – but in terms of vividness, his school days were so engrossing, so absorbing, that they have a clarity more recent times can't match. Six years primary, five years secondary, two years sixth form. It all seemed to pass in slow motion compared to the whip-snap passage of the following years.

When he allows himself, he can still locate people in the seats they took as the register was called in his tutor room. He can remember the answers he gave to questions asked of him before he had reached his teenage years. When pressed, he can describe where he was sitting in a French class when he first heard a certain song playing through earphones concealed in his sleeve.

What use is this knowledge?

Were he able to swap it for aptitude at mathematics he might have achieved so much more than this mere universe.

I must stop him here.

He always returns to this anxiety with maths, but I won't tolerate 'if only'. He never made any effort to develop himself or strengthen the things he was good at; apart from laziness – in this he excelled with Olympic aplomb. Laziness was an illness that ravaged him from the age of eleven.

He could pull off smart, at least when he was young. A top set pupil in everything, until that laziness exposed his weakness in maths. The worst lesson he ever learnt was that it was easier to get in trouble for not doing his school work than to invest the time and effort in actually doing it. Since his twenties, he's cursed himself for this lack of application.

He'll get no pity from me. He has no idea of the huge opportunity he was given. I was offered no school, no curriculum, everything I learnt had to be fought for, had to be stolen from my superiors.

YOU IDIOT.

He's just been online, searching for maths textbooks, infused with the sudden idea that he might manage to right his lack of knowledge and application before he fades away. Fate has led him to an article about Kurt Gödel.

> *By the late 1970s, Gödel's mental health had deteriorated through a growing sense*

*of persecution and paranoia. His wife Adele
cooked all of his meals, but in 1977, when she was
hospitalised for six months, Gödel refused to eat.
He died at Princeton Hospital on 14th January 1978,
with a death weight of 30kg (4 stone 10 pounds –
just over a kilo above the weight Richey Edwards
believed meant unavoidable death in the song '4 st 7 lb').*

What will become of my Creator now that Brina won't be around to ensure that he eats regularly? His starvation is already scheduled. In the meantime he dedicates himself to shovelling any old shit into his mouth.

All this talk of food that he pipes through me.

He is a cruel Creator, though he knows not what he does.

In an act of benevolence, he rewinds time to restore some of the justice owed to me: he has gifted me a freshly dead seabird:

I discover it upon the sand, presented in an ironic foetal curl. A corvine comma with malevolent eyes, feathers stiffened into spines and wings that retain their smooth articulation. I gut it and hang it from the eaves. The blood drip drip drips at slowly increasing intervals. The warm liquid suggests freshness, though nothing dries completely in this humidity. Rich, rusty ichor pools on the sandy clay under the hanging bird; it may be a harbinger of my sustained life, or my imminent death.

The price for my survival is constant vigilance. No one will assist me if I get sick.

My Creator shares the same risk – he has brought about a situation where there is no one to check on him, no one to make sure he gets up if he falls. At some point he will stumble to the ground and the end will begin. Disorientation will lead to a loss of balance, and he will be put to bed.

From there he will lose touch with the world.

The process is written.

He redirects my attention to the bird. Its eyes have clouded and the formerly flexible wings are now frozen in place.

My avian tormentor oppresses me – I have spent too long checking this winged-gift-horse in the mouth, I must pray to my Creator that the food he provides won't kill me.

A cruel trick to play upon a starving man.

§

I woke with my belly full. I am loved.

He keeps returning to me; this gives me strength. He will allow me to tell my story.

Even so, I must keep a close eye on his growing obsession with the songs of his youth and the women he has loved. The introduction of these themes initially struck me as harmless, but I see them growing, cancer-like, dotted throughout this tale.

Mawkish tumours I am powerless to excise.

§

Each day the engine must be warmed up, he must write his way in. The produce of this phase should never see the light of day, though he always hopes that one little pearl might blossom in his cold brain before the flow is found. It is rare, admittedly – most of this early effort is edited away, but one or two ghostly echoes survive to the final draft.

Much of my daily activity has been structured while my Creator 'writes his way in'.

Ghostly echoes.

He scratches away, waits to see what will be revealed.

This morning I must clean my clothes. I'm pragmatic about what cleanliness means – I've never known fabric softeners or brilliant whites. I wash my attire just as our predecessors have for millennia: find a stream, get some rocks and then bash and scrub and bash and scrub, rinse and repeat – all with more care than aggression. Clothes don't last long in the Darien climate.

I make running repairs and put outfits together using combinations of discarded clothing. I'm not ashamed to announce that I have sported the odd ladies' smock, even a couple of dresses in my days alone. I sought to fully indulge the freedom I obtained when freed from society's rigid gender codes, but even with infinite choice in the matter I tend towards traditional male clothing. This is a failure of my imagination.

All things being equal I would spend the dry months naked, as my Creator made me, but there are numerous reasons not to conduct my business in the buff. None of them has anything to do with pride or shame, though I'll be the first to admit to being a sorry specimen in my current state. I've already paid with too much of my skin after cooking in the Darien sun, but there are also biting insects and stinging plants to contend with. We learnt a valuable lesson early on from those who had spent their lives aboard ships – never let the elements in. Wind, rain, sun, snow; exposure to the weather must be carefully managed in order to obtain anything approaching success. The damp here is a fact of life that I can befriend to some extent, but the sun, or the whipped sand carried on the wind; these demand fear and respect.

My Creator has his own issues with damp. A leak in his bedroom snakes down from the roof through the plaster, tracing the lines of the mortar in the brickwork. As the months have passed it has grown more malevolent, spawning a swatch of black mould. Black mould is invariably unhealthy, but Brina turned a blind eye and now that she is gone, my Creator has no interest in addressing it. He will be dead long before his lungs succumb to the mycotoxins. He will bequeath this as an inheritance for the next occupant.

Most people faced with impending darkness feel an obligation to get their house in order, both literally and metaphorically. With the fog of incomprehension closing in, I don't think I can call my Creator slovenly for not doing likewise. He has an entire world to put in order; my future to ensure. Far more pressing than removing mould from a patch of plaster.

Over in his world, there are weeds lifting the terrace slabs, tins of food months out of date, and letters from the bank piled unopened on the kitchen sideboard. None of these demands will ever be addressed, none will be sorted or resolved via the conscious action of my almighty Creator but, by hook or by crook, I am determined to be saved from this cruel spillage of soil, this utter waste of human endeavour.

Perhaps I am condemned to sweet talk him, man to man. *Just fucking save me – get me home.*

Powerless in the face of his own crisis, he can at least settle things up for me. I just have to persuade him of the need for haste, the need to be washed and packed before the shutters slam down.

We've reached the point where it takes him hours to work through a paragraph. He stands, walks the room, thinks of the past, looks through the window, washes his hands, types 'Mozambique' into a search engine, followed by 'Slovene modal verbs'.

These activities are processed by a brain that is less and

less aware of the world. Every so often he'll slump in front of the document that provides my life-support and throw words at it, but his focus can't hold for more than a couple of minutes at a time. He and I are both supremely lucky to have the support of professionals who have a vested interest in this book being finished. His agent is forlorn about the forthcoming demise, but she is keenly aware that you can't buy this kind of publicity. Meetings are taking place in the background, torturous debates surrounding foreign and translation rights. Half respectable figures have been thrown around cafés and offices, at least for a historical novelist with previous sales as piss-poor as my Creator's. I'm booked in for unprecedented attention from my Creator's editor. We both thought this was due to compassion – support in the darkest hours – but it seems the editor is just keen to get started on a project that will require months of work to knock into shape.

A country in Southern Africa with a coastline on the Indian Ocean and land borders with Tanzania, Malawi, Zambia, Zimbabwe, Swaziland and South Africa. Capital city: Maputo (formerly Lourenço Marques). Current flag was adopted on 1st May 1983 and is notable for featuring an AK-47 with bayonet attachment.

My Creator was called away from the desk for a moment.

His mobile phone rang; a number he didn't recognise. He thought it might have been Brina, checking up, though she invariably calls the landline, and he would have recognised the last four or five digits.

The anonymous call has stopped him dead.

His preoccupation with past amours tempted him to think that it might have been Rebecca, calling to arrange a final meeting. A chance to catch up before he went. Say a few things that they'd never managed to voice before, now that somehow they've both managed to grow into proper adults. He could meet her kids. There would be a soft sadness in the air that he would never know fatherhood. They would part without ever admitting what they couldn't bear to say.

I refuse to be the vessel for this.

It was probably a wrong number, some mundane sales call, someone wanting to speak to him about an accident that never happened. He stooped over the coffee table and gazed blankly at the numbers on the screen. Mobile numbers provide no hint of geographical provenance. Why would Rebecca want to see him in this state? Why would he want to let her? He's so broken, so corrupted by fear and illness. He'd shock anyone who'd ever known him in his previous form. Bring her kids – he'd scar them for life.

Perhaps I've been too harsh.

He stood from the desk and faced his image in the hallway mirror, trying to determine if he's as broken as I claim. Once the anxiety faded he began to enjoy just seeing, feeling, recognising. Every moment he must confront the fact that all will soon fade to black.

An instant death is a dream for most of us – with no opportunity to put our houses in order.

In that case, why should he feel any pressure?

§

All these books with which he surrounds himself.

What is to be done about them?

This morning my Creator managed to shuffle his way through a bookshop. He bought a collection of Walser's stories.

When will he read them?

Back at home, he put them on top of the stack he has amassed from his online wish list. What pointless acquisitions.

You can't take it with you.

My endless exhortations exhaust me. We're both so low on energy. Each day I am required to rouse him with stronger words, yet each day we make a little less progress than the last. The diary for next week shows four hospital trips, so the immediate future provides even less opportunity for writing. If I can keep him at the keyboard for longer than ten minutes at a time I consider it a job well done.

As time slips by, the void ahead becomes more welcoming. Perhaps I'm beginning to accept that time is about to run out on us. I'm not capable of sustaining myself once the lights go out. I have a great fear of the loneliness that will come when the light fades and the heat death of my universe rolls in from the Darien horizon. The sky will darken, and for a moment I will think my salvation has come, but I will be forsaken.

I must stop.

My pity is overblown, especially considering the cross my Creator must bear. I don't wish to whip him, to add to the darkness flaying the skin from his ribs.

I want to empathise. I want to reach across the divide and praise his potential. He knows that we are alike, he understands the similarities of our situations.

But of course he knows – this was the plan all along.

Through his keyboard he directs me down dark alleys. We are two men struggling for control of one another. I am made of words and he of matter, yet I am the one who fights for life while he submits to slipping away. He has shut himself off from those who would console him.

He fails to understand that the end of his life touches

others as well. His family, the friends he has left – they need to spend time with him for their own processes of acceptance. They need to work through this terrible thing. But he's no help to them. He has become a mute drone, stumbling, not speaking for days, unable to shepherd the thoughts and images that circulate within his withering mind – a mind that resides in a brain riddled with holes.

Although it doesn't serve me, perhaps his accumulation of books betrays a twisted hope on his part. He might finally be choosing to experience the present. He bought the book today not as something to read in the future, but to enjoy the immediate experience of wanting something and being able to have it.

He has just held the Walser in his hands. It's an attractive edition. The fact that he will never read it, will probably never finish another book, has further fed his sense of the present.

> *A present that sparks and crackles*
> *as my fingers reach out to it.*

In all honesty, he has never sincerely faced the tipping point, now so close by, at which he will no longer sit at his keyboard painting my world. The weight of now is sobering. He meekly accepts that over the next few weeks he will find it ever harder to write. The next stage, so the doctors tell him, will be angry confusion.

After that he will slip below the surface. He will drift from the shoreline of sentience, leave the land of humanity and return to his animal life.

Come, come, I tell him. We were just in the present being constructive. What's with this pessimistic leap into the future?

NO MOPING.

We have a deal.

He is to come back to Darien. We shall take a walk along the beach, past the burning driftwood that keeps me warm in the darkness.

Light the sky. Show me how the sunlight falls on the dunes at the end of the bay.

See how the colour and texture adjust as the sand beneath our feet changes from fine dust to dense clay at the edge of the jungle.

Behind those bushes are the rocks dotted with eggs, guarded by belligerent birds. We can clamber across and onto the narrow plain that runs up to the tree line.

I shall spend today raising your spirits.

§

The missing fragments of time are hard to account for. We both feel it, my Creator and I.

He got off the bed at 8am, took a walk around the block, ate breakfast, checked his mail (0 new messages), brushed his teeth, ambled to the newsagent. Now it's 2pm.

I know the feeling. My days disappear too.

Where does that time go? Even if we turn our backs, close our eyes, jam our fingers in our ears, time still stampedes past. The action of entropy is the only reliable way to mark our movement through space. Even my omniscient Creator doesn't understand what time really is.

With this discovery I lose confidence in him.

Out here in Darien, in the universe he has created, he could invent some definition, some explanation that would satisfy me – something that would tally with the physics and philosophy of this world, but he's broken. There's nothing left in the tank. The bullshit harvest has rotted on the vine.

Quanta of time keep slipping from reach. The intangible

phenomenon that is nonetheless the despot that rules our palpable planet. It is impossible to imagine a world not subject to the passing of time. Cannot be done. No movement, no creation, no destruction: no universe could come to be. A world without time is a nonsense fiction that doesn't warrant a single sentence being wasted on its barren, non-existent soils.

Not like my world.

Not like this Darien of matter, time and repercussions.

I am, therefore I am.

Isn't that enough for a character such as myself?

Created by an all-powerful Creator, I needn't concern myself with the tangibility of the things that surround me. As long as your eyes are scanning these words, I am. I gloriously exist.

What about those moments your mind wanders? I must take that up with my Creator. He must take ultimate responsibility.

Each time he tries to do better.

§

In his condition, it's no wonder he's so obsessed with time.

Time is untrustworthy, deceitful by nature. On occasion I can achieve far more in two hours than two days. Much of the perception of time's passing is a function of coincidence, of things falling into place, finding the flow. It's not possible to work at full capacity at all times: effort, concentration and dumb luck must align. There are those able to take advantage of this alignment more often than others, who pride themselves on their productivity, but they often ignore the role played by luck.

They convince themselves that they have mastered time.

They are wrong.

I lack their enviable ability to make snap decisions. I must think things through, weigh up pros and cons, sleep on it. This is a provocation to those with the ability to make quick choices, those who never realise they live one snap decision from disaster.

My Creator takes a dim view of such individuals.

He sees it as just another roll of the dice. Quick decision making might lie in genetics; just as the tendency to laziness could come from our chromosomes.

My Creator should take some credit for his own attributes. To create a world like mine requires graft. There's room for the merest modicum of talent, but really it's about putting in the hours.

He had time on his hands, so he made me.

There may be no greater purpose, no grander plan.

He lives with the constant fear that he will be found out at any minute.

Imposter syndrome?
But some people really are imposters.

His death sentence is a salvation of sorts: it allows him to fantasise that once he is gone, someone will discover his work and truly understand him. His genius will be revealed.

Nothing humble about this dream, nothing endearing, but perhaps at this late stage I can allow him this one indulgence. Let it slide. I shall feed the delusion if it keeps him stumbling back to Darien day after day. The more obsessed he becomes with aiming at that unattainable perfection, the more likely I am to make it home.

Don't judge me for this pernicious deceit. I need to save myself even if he is well beyond saving. I encourage him to keep doing what he's doing. Keep on the path.

The surest route to our salvation.

§

Not a sound.

Absolute silence.

I hold my breath, beg my heart to still as blood thunders in my head.

Do.

Not.

Move.

Wait.

I'll whisper now that you're around, and liable to draw attention if you're not up to speed. Keep your head down. Look over my left shoulder; there, down by the huts. Those twenty shadows are soldiers in the army of New Granada: Spanish interlopers trampling the sacred soil of New Scotland.

Criminals from Cartagena, trespassing on my patch.

What can I do? I'm nothing in the face of their force. What defence could I possibly mount? Even if the redundant weaponry left by my compatriots was functional, I have no ammunition. I cannot bring a sharpened stick to a flintlock fight.

Everything I possess is down there, everything is on the line.

The one in the most ludicrous hat is clearly in charge, making his way from building to building, surveying and commentating while his sallow companion records his assessment of my mighty Empire.

Stock-taking someone else's property.

Am I not allowed this, my tiny sliver of property on the estate of this great green earth?

When I first returned from collecting roots, I took them to be Kuna hunters taking a look around. They pass through from time to time, expressing indifference and pity. But as I got closer I could make out the blue uniforms with yellow collars.

I have been hiding ever since.

This is dangerous. There's nothing for me to gain from this situation; no compromise, no negotiation. Several of my countrymen were tricked and held by the Spaniards, our ships impounded with impossible ransoms placed upon them. Famously underpaid, the Spanish soldiers are unpredictable. Like bored young men across the planet, in my time and yours, they seek sport, wherever they might find it.

I saw the same in the soldiers we brought to the New World.

Unbloodied blades are a professional affront.

There is nothing to do but to wait for them to leave. There is nothing for them here – as they will soon discover for themselves.

§

They're still here. Perhaps in greater number than before.

And now my stomach calls my tired limbs to action.

There is a primal kinship between hunger and fatigue. I am pinned down, in hiding, and my Creator looks elsewhere.

Brina has been ignoring his calls, or not answering her phone for some reason. Paranoia paints pictures in his mind, tells him stories he cannot bear. It's made him laser focused on heartbreak. He's familiar with this furnace of hurt and humiliation; if he had longer he'd tell himself that he'll emerge a better person for the experience.

No such consolation.

Until these unwelcome interlopers highlighted the inherent insecurity of my solitary state, I have rarely felt endangered by being alone, but I am familiar with the hurt he suffers. Emotional desolation led me on my path to Darien. I was too trusting; I made poor decisions and was unable to show a cold heart to worthless people with wicked intentions.

For this failing, I let down those who mattered most.

Brina's support, through all of his fuck-wittery, melted my Creator's cynicism about love. It had been very different in his younger years with Rebecca. She was always going to be too much for him; that was obvious from the start. And even when he somehow fluked his way into her life, he allowed himself to dream it would be forever – how depressingly adolescent. She was dipping her toe in the waters of relationships, getting her eye in for the future romances that would have real significance. It was an accident that their coupling lasted for years.

A dangerous accident: he began to make plans for their future. He saw the ink drying on their children's birth certificates.

But she had never stopped playing.

She became an adult while he retained the mind of a teenager. His love grew parasitic. Her dreams were full of what the wide world could offer, while his desire was to stay close to their family homes, the same circles, follow his father's career path.

His narrow horizon smothered her. She left.

And now he obsesses upon this theme that he never varies.

Repetition. Repetition – repetition.
A linguistic trigger that always sparks off
the aural memory of Smith's monotonous
incantation from the eponymous reverse-side
of 'Bingo Master's Break-Out!' (1978).

When Rebecca settled down to married life she had never experienced the pain of being the one deserted. Several others came after my Creator, but each time she cut them adrift, leaving a broken man in her wake.

Forgive me for sounding so dramatic – I am condemned to view his history through the warped lens he provides.

Repetition, repetition.

Though, if he wants my opinion, I might agree that Rebecca is missing a vital experience. She can't know the humility that comes from being abandoned by another – forced to learn how to cope with an expected intimacy being withdrawn without warning. She can't understand the feeling of cold distance where shortly before there was warm invitation.

Even as a suddenly single man, there is some comfort for my Creator: he believes Brina will return the calls eventually. He credits her being compassionate enough to drop in for the occasional cup of tea. Although he wishes she could've held on for a few more weeks, deep down he believes she will be available to him until the very end, even if their meetings become awkward.

Better than nothing.

On the other hand, I sense I am destined to never see the face of another woman. If I thought it would sway him I would beg, like he does. I would make promises, strike deals. But that's not for me. He might choose to demean himself by grovelling in the face of hopelessness but I'm too dignified for such a course of action.

It intrigues me that he still finds the emotional space to think about Rebecca. Until his death was thrown in his face, he almost never thought of her. Once or twice a year perhaps, and fleetingly, but she's suddenly become much more significant.

I respect this private emotional rebellion.

And he can be a difficult bugger to respect at times.

Though it angers me that relieving my suffering isn't more of a priority. Of course, I don't curve space-time, but I don't think my concerns should count any less for this fact.

I need some hope of resolution.

I need to prove the bastards wrong.

§

The Spanish leave New Edinburgh for short spells, but they always return. My possessions, such that they are, have been scattered across the square.

History repeating.

When they first left the scene I scrambled towards the huts, desperate to retrieve what I could, but the moment I was about to break cover, raised voices from the path scared me off. The soldiers returned in full force.

Each time they disappear, I inch closer and plan my raid.

Plugging away, doggedly: that's the most important thing to remember.

Perseverance and persistence, these are the attributes we need in the face of everything.

Though it's more than that:

It's about not doubting for a second that you are on the right path. That's the secret to surviving, to creating a world.

Repetition, repetition.

Who am I kidding?

It's all well and good to proclaim that the secret is never doubting, but who throws themselves into any kind of sustained effort without occasionally worrying that the methods or outcomes are not what they intended? Especially when it comes to creating a world: the disconnect between what was imagined and what results is so vast. This struggle has to be about realising the dream as much as possible. Can't ask for more than that.

But the vital truth will be that it is made, that it is extant. Unlike my lunch.

I embrace these stomach pangs, and not just literally. They tell me I am alive. To address my pressing need for food, I've been drying out the fibrous plants that clump around the tree roots. I've established that they aren't poisonous but I'm unsure how much nourishment they might provide. They have crisped in the morning sun and I think the time has come to try a sample.

Not bad. Bitter, but not bad.

This is what I mean by plugging away. I need to keep trying different solutions to my problems. I might be suffering a terrible run of luck and then something will suddenly fall into place. The rough with the smooth. In a few days' time, I will no doubt lie watching the Spanish, listening to the rain, wheezing and starving and my troubles will once again feel insurmountable. But for now, I can see a future.

Is this a life? Dragging myself from hope to despair? My Creator is unsure. When he saw Brina at the weekend she was kind and patient, but it's only a matter of time before he says something that pushes her away again. Ridicule is swiftly delivered, surgically close to the bone and without restraint. His inadequacies announced to the world.

He has only himself to blame.

Perseverance, that's the key.

§

Milestone after milestone.

By my reckoning, today marks a year that I've been here alone. I nearly made the full 365 without company before these Iberian bastards arrived – not bad going for a single-member civilisation on the edge of the known world. I can't be certain, but a year sounds right.

My Creator has been treating me to some particularly clement weather. He's holding me to his bosom for a moment, showing his most wayward sheep some New Testament compassion.

Things have been rough for him this week. Brina's been packing her life into boxes while he sits on the sofa, watching. His possessions are escaping with her. They're both well aware that she's taking plenty of things that they mutually own, but he won't need them in a few weeks, so it seems petty to kick up anything approaching a fuss.

He makes a nest on the sofa and allows the process to swirl around him. He's not going to lose the habit now.

Yesterday, after she'd left, he looked through the CDs to check she hadn't deprived him of anything he might need in the darkening hours

Why does he insist on such triviality?

Especially in a digital world where he has access to everything.

There's so much music that he will never hear again. Same with books. Same with films. What does he care if it all gets caught up in Brina's harvest? There's so much art that he never discovered. That should be the source of his anxiety. Books he will never read; the pillars of cinema of which he will be forever ignorant. Instead my Creator constantly looks back on his narrow life. He's more concerned with the dodgy detritus of Britpop that he accumulated as a teenager than discovering soaring works that would inspire and nourish his final days.

Music. So important to him in his younger iterations, but it lost its pull somewhere in his twenties. What happened there? In his teens there was a tune for every emotional turn, but the whole edifice has fallen into the sea. Now, in his fourth and final decade, he never hears a new song that has that crushing weight, that evocative potential. He can't have 'grown out' of music. What the fuck happened?

But even this isn't true. Music still finds him once in a while, its power seeks him out like a Will-o'-the-wisp at three in the morning after a night on the sauce. The next day his closest friends wake to find social media notifications containing snatches of lyrics or links to music videos that he couldn't bare not to share.

§

Brina came for coffee this afternoon. Their meeting was awkward in that particular way encounters between former lovers often are.

Clipped sentences and talking over each other.

This could have been one of those break-ups that just fades away in quiet sadness, seeing less and less of each other until the cord that connects them finally snaps, but they are held to ransom by the need to get their affairs in order. If he wasn't so exhausted he might spitefully try to run the clock down and leave Brina to deal with the whole mess.

It's probably best that he's too tired for that.

Any hopes he harboured that Brina's visits might become amorous affairs soon faded. The disorder has sapped his libido. He still finds her attractive, but there's no chance he would make a move. The futility of doing so would cause such acute embarrassment they would likely never see each other again. He's understandably keen to avoid clumsy confrontations – I'm glad he has this one grain of self-respect. His desire to prove Brina wrong is one of the main motivations for continuing to work on my world. As long as he has something to prove, he's got a reason to return; so I've no problem with her awkward appearances at the house from time to time.

House-keeping: getting the mundane in order. My Spanish squatters cause me even more aggravation by their presence because I know that my shelter requires repair. There are dark clouds above the hills and the roof is in constant demand of attention. No wonder leaking roofs are fertile ground for proverbs and folk wisdom.

He needs to leave the keyboard to rest every five minutes now. I had hoped things might improve (admittedly within the context of the wider decline), but it's clear we are on the slide. Three or four words strung together feels like a significant struggle. Until recently he could manage a whole paragraph in a single burst, despite the knots it caused in his stomach, but those days are gone.

Stay with me big man, we'll finish this together.

House-keeping.

The enforced abandonment of my to-do list.

The Spaniards are also keeping me from tending to the crude fishing nets I've constructed from discarded clothing. They're difficult to use and don't yield a great amount, but the few times they've worked are enough to keep me trying. I can see them draped in the trees nearest the sea line, unmolested by the interlopers but slowly being ravished by neglect.

My exile to the fringes of the colony is wasting the other skills I have developed while living by myself. I can collect fresh water and keep it potable for several days. I can manage my sanitary waste satisfactorily. I can pluck, skin and gut many different animals when the opportunity arises. But without tools or the liberty to use my land, none of this matters.

A Darien of one's own.

By ensuring my ongoing survival, even with my current deprivations, I feel I must be holding up my end of the bargain.

§

The snap of a branch. I'm awake.

Two Spanish soldiers swipe absently at the bush that conceals me. I don't understand their words, but the tone expresses boredom. I mustn't move, I mustn't make a sound. They're a yard at most from my prone body, and discovery would mean instant death.

I try not to breathe; scrunch my face into the mossy earth and sip air against the cool ground.

This situation is intolerable.

The invaders will not cease, will not change course, will not, frankly, fuck off from my life.

I must remedy their error in coming to my land.

Enough is enough. Once I discover where they are based, I must drive them out.

The sound of my tormentors is fading. They must be retreating. Rather than using this opportunity to retrieve my possessions, I rise and creep in the direction of their voices. I can cut out a lot of the work by following a route broadly south – in the direction of their settlements in this region.

Their sound drifts away. I am heading in the wrong direction. Cut back.

There they are, but heading north?

Yes, they are between me and the sea, and unquestionably heading north.

This doesn't make sense.

I follow them for forty minutes. The undergrowth is sparse around the tree trunks and I am easily able to keep up while maintaining a safe buffer between us. When the trees break into a clearing, I pause and let the soldiers continue.

The sight ahead sickens me.

Rows of tents stretch out across an incline and several acres of forest have been cleared. An engineering project is underway with a permanent intention.

This cannot be permitted to happen. The Spanish have a vast empire to the south of Darien, I cannot allow them to cut me off from the sea.

Shit.

This is what happens when one is passive in the face of fortune.

Take what you want, I won't need it.
If it's not hers, help yourself.

Please, take anything, he said to his parents, his cousin, the neighbours.

He meant it at the time.

But now they're here, in his space, asking him about this and that – things he doesn't care about. People appear in the periphery of his world, asking how he is, then sizing up his assets. He wishes they'd take the lot and go, leave him be. Stop burdening him with their presence.

§

In my exile, I wander the narrow hinterland that connects me to New Edinburgh.

This afternoon I am walking in the area known as Alca, said to mean 'bones of men' in the local language. I am drawn to the sombre poetry of the territory's name.

The going is tough, the settlement was abandoned long ago and vegetation has reclaimed any paths that might once have linked it to the rest of the region.

As the scrub thins out, a small plain sweeps out to the base of the hills.

I trip on something lodged in the loose soil and fall to the ground.

Seeking the cause of my fall I find an ivory humerus protruding from the soil.

I pause; the malnourished mind is prone to playing tricks.

On my knees, I dust at the ground, and glide my fingers over the unmistakable web of bones that form a human hand.

I gingerly remove my left heel from a jawbone, still equipped with a few shiny molars.

I pull a femur loose and clutch it, disbelieving.

The ground is more bone than soil.

I freeze, suddenly terrified that the valley of bones is a hunting ground: the field of war for a formidable beast that would make swift work of my flimsy body.

The bones are clean and the ground dry dust, but the stench of death sinks upon me. I recognise the smell – the scent arrived with the first cases of flux during our voyage. The vapour of life dragged from another that sticks in throat and troubles the soul.

I rise to my feet and stumble blindly into the undergrowth.

I run and run.

I pass through the forest and slip into the clearing around New Edinburgh, back to the scores of Scottish dead buried deep. The Spaniards are thankfully absent.

I cross into the square with a pounding heart and sink to my knees.

In spite of the graves, this precarious peninsula is the closest thing I have to a safe haven on this side of the Atlantic.

I clutch my head in my hands and realise with revulsion that I am still holding the femur.

I throw the bone to the ground and stagger back to the safety of the treeline.

§

My Creator has been unearthing some bones of his own and it makes him uneasy. Brina has moved out, de facto; yet she keeps dropping by. It often takes him time to notice if someone else is in the building. He'll freeze motionless, in the centre of the kitchen, attempting to establish what goal might have led him there. These are the thoughts that form his mental life. While trying to reorient himself

Reorient or reorientate?
Both from the French to organise to face East,
but why not reoccident?

his eyes almost always settle on some painful remnant of his ruined relationship. In more proactive times he would have erased every shred of evidence that the building once housed another person, someone he loved.

I gnaw away and remind him I'm his only hope.

Think of the potential, I whisper, set us both free. He could save his reputation. He can't become a great, there's not the talent for that, but why not aspire to being a curate's scrambled egg? We might strike a chord with someone, somewhere.

*Momčilo Gavrić was the youngest soldier
in the First World War. After his family
was killed by Austro-Hungarians and his house
was burned down, he was taken in by
the 6th Artillery Division of the Serbian Army.
He was promoted to Corporal following
the Battle of Cer in August 1914.
He was eight years old.
Assume he outranked some adults?*

We have nothing to lose.

He's just returned to the keyboard. He'd stood, flicked through the sparse scattering of CDs that remain on the shelf, thought about the times he and Brina would drunkenly dance at four in the morning. At some point one of them would notice the blue of dawn seeping in at the edge of the curtains.

THOSE DAYS ARE GONE.
Come back to becoming life, the creator of worlds.

I am roused by Spanish shouts.

I rise to my knees and watch from behind my bush.

They are armed. They shout into the forest.

Soon they will come in my direction. I crawl back into the thickening woods, further into the darkness.

I can see their leader brandishing the femur that I had discarded in the square.

Behind him, two men are struggling with a large object.

They sling the awkward bundle outside one of the buildings. It is a body dressed in Spanish uniform.

Carelessly dropped, clearly dead.

The captain gesticulates with the femur, directing his men with the macabre baton.

I stare hard at the distant grey oval of the dead man's face.

It wasn't me. I didn't kill him. I would have mentioned such a transgression. My Creator would have demanded that I confess to such a crime in these pages.

Over the next couple of hours the Spanish pack up their possessions and leave, taking their dead comrade with them.

I wait for three days in the bush before I decide it is safe to return to New Edinburgh.

They do not return.

§

Back to business.

Prior to the diagnosis my Creator was beginning to worry that he was getting too old to 'arrive' as a significant writer. It concerned him that he might be too long in the tooth, past it, too unattractive to major publishers. To his credit, he takes responsibility for his lack of achievement. The greatness that held such significance to his younger self was always going to elude him. The Beatles were done and dusted long before they reached his age. They arrived barely out of adolescence and changed popular music forever, before collapsing into a slough of spent creativity.

I was the walrus…

The twenty-seven club: all those singular talents snuffed out before their thirties; look at Rimbaud. My Creator wasted too much of his teens and twenties, a grubby boy too preoccupied with his penis and easily acquired animal pleasures.

He did nothing to be considered worthy of these omni-potent powers of creation.

The universe knows no justice.

None of this is relevant anymore. I implore him to back away from regret, spurn sentimentality.

> *Aged eighteen, Mathias Rust*
> *dreamt of bridging the Iron Curtain.*
> *On 13th May, 1987, with a mere fifty hours'*
> *flying time and a rented Cessna, he took off*
> *from Uetersen. First, he visited*
> *the Faroe Islands en route to Iceland.*
> *After a week there he flew to Bergen;*
> *seemingly on his way home to Germany.*
> *However, on the morning of the 28th May,*
> *Rust flew to Helsinki and refuelled his plane.*
> *Shortly after take-off, Rust disengaged*
> *all communication equipment and disappeared*
> *from Finnish radar. Search and rescue operations*
> *began immediately. Rust's aeroplane appeared on*
> *Soviet military radar. Rust was tracked by*
> *surface-to-air missile batteries. Two fighter jets*
> *scrambled to intercept the unidentified craft.*
> *For some reason, permission to engage was*
> *never granted, surely saving the teenager's life.*
> *In the early evening, he appeared*
> *above central Moscow. His intention*
> *to land in Red Square proved impractical*
> *due to the large number of bystanders.*
> *He landed on a nearby bridge,*
> *before taxiing to a halt close to the square.*
> *Rust signed autographs for*

Gifted seemingly limitless quantities of time, motivation can become a real issue for someone with the psychological apparatus of my Creator. When there's always a tomorrow, most tasks can be put off indefinitely. He weeps at the memory of so many wasted weekends, so many idle moments, so many hours watching television to which he was indifferent at best. If he'd known the cruelty of his future, he would have achieved so much more.

But I am thankful that, even in this indistinct and belated sense, his impending demise has flung him into my world.

bewildered locals before
being arrested two hours later.
Sentenced to four years in a labour camp,
Rust served less than a year
in a detention centre before being released
as a goodwill gesture to the West
during a period of warming relations.
Journalists described Rust as
'psychologically unstable and unworldly
in a dangerous manner'.

It feels almost spiritual, the way he selflessly dedicates himself to my cause. I'm still surprised that he hasn't renounced his atheism and embraced religion; but then, with his life-giving abilities, he has no need of a higher power.

I believe.

Oh, never you worry about my spiritual health – I believe alright.

I'm in direct communion with my Creator. I know his mind, his mumbling. Perhaps I have the right to consider myself a messiah of sorts?

Rebecca had no wisdom teeth.
Not that they've been removed,
they were never there.

How do we spring from our mistakes to make something, to leave a mark? Most of us wrestle with this problem from time to time, but my Creator ponders it ceaselessly. This noble preoccupation leads me to resolve that if I am saved, I shall make a positive difference to the lives of those to whom I return. My marooning has focused my mind. Like my Creator, I am drawn to analysing the mistakes I have made, the opportunities wasted, the times I could have been more generous or less selfish. My memories parade my worst before me; I must endure a show-reel of shame before my mind gives me access to my best moments. I have tried to be a good man, failing more often through thoughtlessness or laziness than any kind of bad behaviour. But, at the end of the day, the motive fades away. Others will never know your true motives; but your deeds and actions are plain to see.

This brings to mind a tale I once heard in Greenock. I saw a leathery creature slumped in the street having been banished from a drinking den, neither drunk nor insensible, but soon set upon by the local urchins. I chased the children from the scene and the old man beckoned to me.

He said he had a story:

A man was watching a river flow when a child poured into view, struggling against the current. The man looked around for someone to save the child but there was no one to be found.

Soon another child appeared, thrashing more violently than the first. The man on the bank became desperate. He was no hero; he would never be able to save both children, and he knew that further downstream the river whipped into a wild white torrent. His pulse pounded in his ears. Then it came to him: the action outweighs the motive a hundred-fold. He cast his bundle aside and threw himself into the river.

I asked the man if the hero from the river survived, if he saved the children.

He spat at my feet, called me an imbecile.

I assured him I meant no offence.

I am the man from the river, he roared, don't you recognise a hero when one sits before you?

I left him to the urchins, the hour was late and I had no business in that part of town once darkness arrived. But his tale caught on my mind. I resolved that I was morally bound to hurl myself into the river at any point. I had never heard a more sensible course of action.

§

Note to editor: a scheme for the numbered parts saved unsecured on this memory stick is to be found in the drawer beneath the printer. 'Brina' knows where it is if you have trouble finding. I have also included hand-written notes that are unlikely to suffice verbatim, but must be included in the given order. Again, 'B' can explain further.

Now that the Spanish have departed, the Kuna have reappeared – miraculously rematerialising once I've done all the hard work. A couple of tribesmen visited, but our interactions exchange a frustratingly small amount of information. Within the colony, language learning was only undertaken by a couple of self-selected scholars; the rest of us weren't invited to participate. The lingua-franca of the region is Castilian, but only the most basic elements have been bestowed upon my brain. I should have an aptitude for language learning, if given enough exposure. As a girl, my mother sang some Norn, knew Gaelic and lived in English; but only this last tongue was passed on to me.

Although my Creator could declare me fluent in the language of the Kuna at the sweep of his keyboard, today he is unwilling to make my life so easy. All plot is conflict, he tells me.

Do he and I not have enough conflict to contend with? I can only assume his cruelty springs from his own struggles with Slovene – despite myriad opportunities to learn.

All these missed chances.

He had peers who finished their comprehensive education able to communicate competently in French or German. There was no such achievement for my Creator. He could never find the melody; never get the feel of another language. He could get comfortable with reading, where he could take his time, crank his feeble mind into gear, but listening, writing, speaking – these skills are forever out of reach. Language acquisition has eluded him, just as musical ability did.

Escaping these failures, he has committed himself to the mischievous creation of worlds and beings where everything will work as he wishes.

The disruptive part of the rhythm section,
running interference
on a perfectly proficient drummer.

I shouldn't show anger towards him, it will be a distraction. I make a rod for my own back. My unkind analysis from the previous paragraph merely made him leave the screen to pore over his Slovene exercise books, see if he can't squeeze a little more of the language into his withering mind. He's even booked a lesson for two days' time – can you imagine such a thing? He offends me by suggesting that he's been spending too much time in Darien, causing him to neglect his study of Slovene.

He seems keen to persist in this most futile of tasks.

I want Brina to return, she could save him from this madness. I'm willing to strike a deal: I am prepared to permit him some small serving of life away from me, I'm not a monster. I want him to get in touch with those he cares for but hasn't seen for years, but I don't see the point in a terminally ill man learning the language of a country to which he will never return.

It's clearly another way to distract himself. He keeps pulling Slovene textbooks from the shelves. The fact that I am his last chance is ignored as he attempts to familiarise himself with the differing positions of clitics in various Slovene sentences.

> *By volunteering to be imprisoned undercover*
> *in Auschwitz, Witold Pilecki was instrumental*
> *in proving to the Allies that the Holocaust*
> *was happening. Already mobilised as a soldier*
> *before the outbreak of war, Pilecki and his commander,*
> *Jan Włodarkiewicz, had a distinguished*
> *military record when they established*
> *the Secret Polish Army in November, 1939.*
> *Little was known about the Auschwitz camp*
> *in 1940. In order to gather intelligence,*
> *Pilecki presented a plan to infiltrate the camp*
> *and organise resistance against the institution*
> *from within. Equipped with a false identity card,*
> *Pilecki was swept up by Nazi street patrols*
> *in September 1940 and sent to the camp.*
> *There he survived pneumonia to organise*
> *the Union of Military Organisations, which soon*
> *became the umbrella resistance organisation*
> *within the death camp. The movement was also*
> *responsible for a secret radio station*
> *that broadcast reports from the camp during 1942.*
> *What's Polish for 'balls'/'cojones'?*
> *More vital to the overall progression*
> *of the war were the detailed reports compiled*
> *by Pilecki and smuggled out. By March 1941,*
> *these were making it to the British Government.*

When this glut of intelligence was met
with constant postponements of action by the Allies,
Pilecki decided that the time had come to escape.
Equipped with a bundle of stolen documents,
he and two comrades silenced a guard,
cut the phone lines and departed
the camp on 27 April 1943.

I want him to stop fucking with me – it breaks my heart, enough to fall to my knees and weep.

I shake with the rage of impotence and slump forwards into the dry sand.

After the war, Pilecki fell afoul of
the ruling Soviet authorities.
Sent to work undercover by the Polish
government-in-Exile, he was hung out to dry
by that administration when they conceded
the hopelessness of their situation.
Pilecki's identity was revealed, but he refused to leave
and was subjected to a show trial.

Jądra

Pilecki was executed on 25 May 1948.

He can't let the universe shut its door on me just because that is what's happening to him. He is all powerful. There is not one problem of his own making that he can't solve in my world. No matter how implausible the plot contrivance, there can be a smooth resolution if he deems it so.

SAVE ME. SAVE US.

He no longer knows what to do – he's angry at me, like a true Creator. I am his guilt – his nagging sense of potential unfulfilled and time wasted. From this I take comfort – he is angry because we will be together until the bitter end, when the last drops of conscience and comprehension dribble from the corner of his mouth onto the hospital pillow.

He doesn't know what to do now – I've derailed his train of thought.

BEFORE IT'S TOO LATE.

Something thuds on the sand next to me, heavy and substantial.

Two books, two volumes. I read the title: Slovar slovenskega knjižnega jezika. Razumem – I understand completely – a comprehensive Slovene dictionary. I can speak Slovene.

I believe.

§

This will be the last Christmas.

The last festive season.

The last new year.

The last supper.

It's going to be a painful couple of weeks for my Creator. He's made plans to spend the time with his parents; I think that's reasonable, as long as he takes his laptop. He's been prescribed so many drugs the suitcase is already half full. I'm impressed by the optimism of modern medicine. All I need to do is cut my foot in the stream and I'm confined to my hovel, shivering and sweating, worrying I won't make the morning. One dodgy shellfish and I find myself feebly scooping a pit in the sand to contain the torrent of vomit. To hear my Creator's friends and loved ones speak it sounds as if there is a cure for almost anything.

Almost anything.

My Creator hurls a heavy wave onto the shore and the salty spray whips my chops.

Almost anything. I accept that there is no cure for Prionic Fatal Insomnia.

I must remember – best not to anger him when he's

indulging a sentimental Christmas trip.

I can't blame him, not really. His sense of Christmas is inextricably bound with memories of childhood and the poignant dwindling of the number of relatives as the years passed. He had always imagined that he would be responsible for raising the numbers again by starting a family of his own, but with Brina gone and his death in the post, there's no chance of that.

> *Omayra Sánchez – can't get Frank Fournier's*
> *photo of her out of my mind. It's the eyes.*
> *The head and shoulders of a normal*
> *thirteen-year-old girl stares at us,*
> *as if treading water in a pool,*
> *while the rest of her is pinned under the debris*
> *of her home, destroyed in the landslide.*
> *The photo online – eyes holding the camera's gaze*
> *at the end of the three days during which*
> *the world watched her die. There's stoicism,*
> *but the photo looks like it's taken*
> *shortly after she knows the game's up,*
> *the pain is too great and she is showing*
> *that she knows so much more than any of us.*
> *Privileged knowledge for her alone.*

He's asked his relatives not to give him presents, I think that's fair. What would they get him? He'll be doing fantastically if he makes it to February with the ability to recognise his direct family. I hope his request was sincere – I sense some self-pity sneaking in and it wouldn't surprise me if he secretly hoped for gifts regardless of his request. A short while ago he stopped a couple of feet from the front door, sat on the doormat and cast his mind back across all of his Christmases past. He wanted to remember the earliest that remained. There were flashes of an event when he must have been five or six, there were presents, but it may have been a birthday; through the window he could see the front garden in Bourton Avenue and the sun was shining. The Christmases of his younger years are far more distinct than those of more recent times – there was no drinking as a child, and Christmas was infused with hyper-reality to his young eyes. Everything about the day was unbearably exciting. Most of all, he was excited about being given *things*. There are no more passionate advocates of consumerism than children at yuletide.

He has always told himself that he managed to opt out of that acquisitive inclination; he became sanctimonious about it. He never felt a need to have the latest phone, a modern car or expensive electrical goods. But the books, I remind him. Look around. He considered himself immune to materialism, but there are books everywhere, on the shelves, in piles on the floor, on every table. They are all the result of commerce.

> *The other photo that haunts is that of 'Green Boots'.*
> *It's not got the raw empathy of Sánchez's image,*
> *but bewilderment at the fact that no one*
> *is certain who the alpine-clothing clad corpse is.*
> *There are several theories, but it baffles*
> *that there is a dead body on a hillside*
> *that will never be recovered.*
> *Indeed, Green Boots is a landmark.*
> *A macabre milestone for those dragging themselves*
> *through the atmosphere to the peak of Everest.*
> *Such frank sadness to the solitude.*
> *Lonely end.*

I consider books to be a luxury. The scripture left by my fleeing compatriots cannot survive the local humidity, but amongst my possessions I have a copy of Euclid. I keep it for the quietest of moments, allowing myself to covetously bask in pride at the quality of its construction. It is folded in leather, which protects it from the elements and provides a tactile pleasure in the hand, but there is precious little inside to offer comfort to an abandoned man. Cold geometry; there are no hopes or dreams within its pages. If the sun is shining, then I am pleased by the harmony of shapes and their relationships, but I have to project this beauty upon the material. I can't begin to understand the lion's share of what I read between those sturdy leather covers.

Playing it safe is a risky business.

I miss Christmas. It never meant a day off for me or my neighbours, but it is the greatest of the feast days. There's generosity and charity in the air. In the middle of the unremitting fight with nature that we call winter, it's important not to pass up on an opportunity for human warmth. When I think of the wind and snow of home, I'm tempted to praise my Creator for marooning me on this isthmus. For all the struggles I endure against the natural world, there will be no ice in Darien.

I shan't hold a mass here – I'm still scarred by the tyranny of Campbell and Drummond at the last Christmas of the colony. The rest of us were cowed by mortal terror. No Christian care or compassion in evidence that day. Every one of us expected a Spanish attack at any moment and our leaders fuelled us with fear, convincing us to further shed our humanity in preparation for war.

Perhaps, now alone, I will entirely forgo Christmas this year; it will be a day like any other instead of a painful reminder I can ill endure.

§

An ominous milestone: yesterday was the first day that he was unable to write anything. He lay on his bed, staring at the ceiling. For the first five hours of the day he watched sunlight and shadow slide across the wall and listened to the sounds of the neighbourhood. I'd break through the silence every now and again, but I was unable to coax him into action. His phone shivered as messages arrived, but he left them unread, unconsidered. The darkness is creeping in and I'm going to have to fight him even harder. The scans of his brain show increasing patches of blank space; the doctors have stopped sharing the detailed results with him and my Creator pretends to be too dumb to ask.

I want him to be proud of our shared secret – the fact that everyone thinks he spends his time at the laptop chronicling his condition. He has mentioned a last novel to Brina and his parents, but none of them think he's really neglecting to record the experience of navigating his personal path through Prionic Fatal Insomnia. Why should they be so dismissive of his dedication to prose fiction – what other vehicle would be more appropriate for recording his steady descent into unceasing mindlessness?

> *Why the unquestioning attachment to non-fiction?*
> *Why the elevation of factual writing?*
> *All words are filtered through the mind*
> *of the producer; a creative decision about*
> *what to include, what to omit.*

When Brina and his family finally discover me, I've no doubt they'll feel an acute sense of betrayal. I will be met by people shaking with rage at the lack of answers. I need to be the first witness called in my Creator's defence: on his own terms, he recorded the experience of someone stricken in this terrible way.

But my pleading won't be enough; they will be searching for a more literal account. The odd person might permit a wry smile at the metaphor I represent, but for those in search of true insight there's nothing to learn, no source material for academic papers.

What about my life – aren't there lessons to be found here? He is, after all, a prose writer. Why should my experience be considered inadequate just because people want to learn directly from my Creator's suffering? Humanity has done precious little to learn from any of the other books that came before this one. The moral guidance of the Bible soon gave way to dogma and manipulation; even the vast wealth of medical literature goes unheeded – how many cigarettes are smoked in a day? People don't really want to learn. Fuck them. Give them stories instead.

Talking of cigarettes, he smoked again the other day. Long time since he gave them up, but he thought he'd give it a go again, for old time's sake. Did nothing for him. Even when terminally ill he couldn't retrieve that old excitement for the taste of Golden Virginia.

> *Tommy Brown was one of the three men*
> *who boarded a German U-boat in 1942*
> *and retrieved the enigma codes, playing a pivotal*
> *role in cracking the German communications*
> *and swinging the war in the Allies' favour (hyperbolic?).*
> *The only one of the trinity who climbed aboard*
> *to survive, his fame soon spread,*
> *meaning his true age became known (sixteen).*
> *This was below the minimum age requirement*
> *of seventeen, so Brown's posting to his ship was withdrawn.*
> *He became the youngest recipient of the George Medal.*
> *Tommy Brown died attempting to rescue*
> *his sister from a house fire in 1945.*

That spark of relief that his brain expressed, knowing that soothing nicotine was on the way. It just struck him as pungent and pointless. There are far more diverting indulgences he could be entertaining; he's come round to making the most of the internet.

I mustn't cast the first stone. Even by myself, all the way out here, I'm subject to the more animal urges. I was raised believing that onanistic attention led to severe divine judgement, but being privy to my Creator's habits I know I may self-abuse with impunity.

Back to him, for he insists. Flat in bed, blinking at the ceiling; thinking, listening, but not doing anything, not eating, not drinking, not writing. It scares me when I know what's to come. It's going to be hard to say goodbye, and not just because I depend on him for my entire being.

That's exactly why I can't abide him lying in bed like a dumb animal. He's spent too much time on his back, nursing hangovers and snoozing through the entire weekend. Repetition. He let life wash over him. Repetition. He'd better take the opportunity to tear off a big chunk before it's finished with him. I'm no doctor, but I reckon he's got a month of actually being able to do things of his own free will. If he really concentrates, he can thread a needle. It might take ten minutes, but it's possible. His motor skills are on the wane, but his mind's still holding up. The short term memory is less than sound, but throw some words in front of him and he can soar – instantly finding form and sense. I must convince him that Darien is a place of comfort; a safe space. No one and nothing can get to him here. I cling to this deal we make hour after hour: I'll provide somewhere to think, somewhere to create, just save me, get me out of here before the end.

Repetition.

It's a fair proposal, but deep down I know I'm in no position to make deals with my Creator.

> *Libero Grassi wasn't precociously young,*
> *but he deserves to have made a mark.*
> *A clothing manufacturer in Palermo,*
> *One day in 1990, Grassi decided that*
> *he'd had enough of paying*
> *the Mafia protection money.*
> *He wrote an open letter to his extortionists*
> *which was published in a local daily.*
> *Initially the local mayor, court officials,*
> *head of police and local press*
> *travelled to his factory to show support.*
> *Grassi became a modest national hero.*
> *Other local business leaders lacked Grassi's courage.*
> *They left him high and dry;*
> *his workers were subjected to threats*
> *and intimidation. His shop was broken into*
> *and the previously demanded sum was stolen.*
> *In late August, 1991, Libero Grassi*
> *was shot in the head three times.*
> *He was sixty-seven.*

§

As his tired mind drags, he is capturing the words that come to him anywhere he can, opening old documents and throwing new text in amongst the old. I fear for the person required to trawl through the electronic palimpsest he will leave seared upon the hard drive. He writes instructions on a succession of sticky pad notes and old envelopes and pins them to the board above his desk, but it's a hospital pass. I'm moved to admire the fact that he retains the hubris to do such a thing, to believe that someone will have the time to go through and decipher.

§

I'm becoming abundantly aware of how much the times are a-changing. Life drains away quicker each day, and my Creator spends much of it looking through the window. I'd claim he watches the world, but his mind is blank. Everything outside is just so much flashing light. When lucid thoughts do fall upon him, he returns to me and what I represent – the unfulfilled potential, the glory he will never taste. This is when I hold him to my breast and stroke his hair. That's right, I say, stay here with me. Everything will be fine, don't go back there, to the uncertainty and darkness. Stay here. They will disappear and we can become everything.

He doesn't listen to me as much as he should.

There is still a tradition in Flanders:
Each year one prisoner is released
and pardoned, on the condition that they
walk to Santiago de Compostela
bearing a heavily weighted bag
and accompanied by a guard.
Santiago de Compostela is
1,742km from Bruges.
Google estimates 360 hours.
Does this mean the guard must take the pilgrimage as well?

He understands how painful this must be for his family, though he fails to act on this knowledge. For all I know, his mother and father are still in the room, but he hasn't moved his head for hours and I can only know what he knows. They are ignored; they are punished for their own gift of creation.

His meals remain uneaten on the table. He shuffles absently from room to room, rarely making it from one door to the next without stopping.

Brina's departure is to be celebrated – we both understand that now. She was never going to be able to cope with this new phase. Were she here, he would be entirely dependent upon her; now he is forced into independence. She was always open about her desire not be burdened with children and yet he has taken the withered form of an oversized toddler. She would not be able to support such a creature.

She is gone and

> *Tuone Udaina is notable*
> *thanks to eavesdropping on his parents.*
> *He was the last living person*
> *to speak the Dalmatian language,*
> *which he picked up from ma and pa.*
> *The linguist Bartoli*
> *travelled to the island of Krk*
> *to record Udaina's knowledge*
> *of the language in 1897.*
> *Udaina was killed in an industrial*
> *explosion the following summer.*
> *The Dalmatian language died with him.*

the house is still.

His parents leave food out for him when they go. It's difficult for me to know how much time they spend here, my Creator ignores them. Perhaps 'ignore' is a poor choice of word, it makes him sound ungrateful. He is appreciative of the fact that they want the best for him, but as his brain cracks and fades he is undergoing a process of disengagement with everyone. This means he must let his parents slip away, along with everything else he has gathered over the years.

The people who have passed through his life are washed out memories. They are like images printed onto paper and thrown into a fire. The flame catches, creeps across the faces and leaves the shape of the paper intact until it flakes to ash. The pieces will never be reconfigured, reconstituted. They are lost to the universe, just as the material reality of my Creator will be lost to the mere memories of others. Soon he will only remain as the afternoon thought of an old friend stuck in traffic, a face glimpsed in a crowd, a witty phrase misremembered, an odd act of kindness, some useful advice. Whenever Brina feels a breeze on her back she will remember his rebuke about the dangers of uncovered kidneys.

Tsutomu Yamaguchi survived.
That's why we know about him.
He was famous for being a double hibakusha
– someone affected by the explosion.
No one ever says they should have spent more time
at work when they lie on their deathbed.
Tsutomu Yamaguchi more than most, probably.
He was on business in Hiroshima
on 6th August 1945.
That's when the bomb hit.
Little Boy.
In spite of his injuries, his dedication to duty
made him return to his home town
of Nagasaki the next day.
He returned to work in the city on 9th of August.
That's when the second bomb hit.
Fat Man.
A man in a pub once said of another punter:
If he fell in a barrel of tits
he'd come out sucking his thumb.

He must be careful; I'm growing wise to his games. The curtain slips too often. I see the whirring machinery, the blueprints and drawing boards. He no longer cares for realism at this late hour. My rescue could have come at any moment, indeed, I could have walked through the trees behind me and emerged in central Edinburgh, but that won't happen. A flying craft could carry me across the seas back to the bosom of my family, but that won't happen either.

No deus ex machina will drop from the ceiling and save either of us. Not because fiction is unable to sustain such a thing, but because my Creator and I are such abominable works of fiction that justice won't permit it.

I am tired of talking, and you must be tired of listening.

I am tired of Pilate pursuing me along this coastline, draped in elaborate robes and demanding to know: what is truth?

If I stop to consider my answer he cackles and kicks sand in my face.

I am tired of this trip.

You plagiarist, I scream in Pilate's face, no longer able to abide the constant hounding, you let other men put words in your mouth.

He rolls with belly laughter and sweeps his arms over the sea. He beckons to the birds and the beasts, the trees and the sky.

Behold the man, he demands of them.

My Creator is tired of all of this.

§

Disengagement has become something of a theme.

Knocks at the door go unanswered, phone chirrups ignored, emails unopened.

I indulge a fantasy that my Creator and I are holed up in this together, alone – but the outside world persistently attempts to intrude.

The spell is fragile and easily broken.

A constant reminder that I am always one remove from any other person. I am disengaged by default.

SM-046 (out of respect for privacy).
A woman who suffered from
Urbach-Wiethe disease and had complete
bilateral amygdala destruction in childhood.
Resulting in an inability to feel fear or anxiety.
In many ways this has been A BAD THING.
It appears she has been subjected to many
acts of crime and life-threatening experiences.
She has received explicit death threats.
Is this because people are enraged by her lack of fear?
Or does her condition make her hard work?

Unwittingly, he has allowed his disengagement to cloud the days, acting as a rare soporific. Now that the end is near, he wishes he had been more vigilant, rather than indulging his memories.

He worries he should have been participating in the physical world.

Spending time with the people who hold him dear.

People who will be left bereft by his departure.

Of course, his investing all of his time in the physical world would've been suicidal for me. I couldn't have lived the life I have lived if he was dedicated to his present, his world of people, of society. Now that he can't get that time back, I can show boundless sympathy. I can afford to tell him that if we had our time again I would demand that he engage and enjoy himself in his final months – it costs me nothing to demonstrate such reasonable behaviour.

He can't take anything back.

He can't metaphorically climb aboard the ship and abandon me on the shore. Instead, he and I have mutinied against life, setting sail on our own ship, crewed by the two of us, headed for the precipice that marks the end of the world.

If only he'd realised, I call to him, crackling through the bursts of mental distortion that repossess his mind.

If only my Creator had understood the implications of squatting in this internal life.

Agonising over people, plots and places that exist only in his mind.

He might have pulled so much more from the wreckage of his life.

Hindsight is a wonderful thing, but he lived as a child, too simple to absorb the lessons.

Even when those lessons were easily packaged within popular culture. The drum and bass track that saw heavy rotation at his teenage house parties sampling Matthew Broderick's Ferris Bueller breaking the fourth wall, telling him to look around every now and again, else he might miss life sprinting by.

He didn't hear the message. He didn't listen.

Why pay attention to such a clichéd piece of hokey, homespun wisdom?

How much real wisdom is one exposed to at teenage house parties? Back then he was naïve enough to think that they accurately represented how adults lived.

When their parents were absent they wholeheartedly embraced their freedom.

The 'free house' was the most prized occasion of their young lives.

They drank and smoked and danced and fucked and learnt of things they'd never even known existed.

He didn't understand that this wasn't the beginning but the pinnacle of the closeness they would share.

He was unable to appreciate how fleeting the time would be. To him, this was the future, how life would be forever.

The delusion persisted, for a while.

The rented properties of university stretched his social net, but real life crept in with paid employment.

Jobs and career ambitions offer a different form of liberation, one understood in the narrowest of terms.

> *A warped mirror that distorted*
> *the freedom of the past.*

My Creator had been with Rebecca throughout sixth form, university and into the world of work, but entrance into this new environment led her away on a path through the forest that wasn't accessible to him.

> *'Imagining the blue plaque above the place*
> *I first ever touched a girl's chest.'*
> *Incessant mental soundtrack as fingers*
> *slipped under clothing. Early evening,*
> *escape from a party, breath sour with red wine.*
> *Bench on a triangle of grass, just up*
> *from the train station.*

She reneged on their promises while he was looking the other way.

Her post-doctoral role led her to the type of men with whom she had pictured sharing her life all along.

She had no desire for a Creator of worlds; she wanted a maker of homes.

Builder of furniture.

Contributor of sperm.

My Creator was cast from the garden.

Why does he tell me all this?

The phone is ringing again, but he's trapped too far

inside himself.

Continue this splendid isolation.

Even minded to answer the call, his ability to quickly move to another room has long deserted him.

Sentences are arduously pulled from his mind, each paragraph forming over hours and subject to continuous revision.

Everything is toil.

He'll soon turn his back on me as Rebecca and Brina did to him.

I don't deserve such treatment.

I was never stupid enough to think we promised our futures to each other.

How I sting him.

All I mean is: when it comes to the relationship he and I share, I have always brought the maturity to know that nothing lasts forever.

Nothing ever lasts forever.

Since he created me with the express intention of stranding me on Darien, I have been living on borrowed time.

I've no hope of forever.

Forever. Such a potent concept to the sentimental teenager.

One of the first things cast aside by any adult worth their salt.

Honest with ourselves, we are forced to live with the fact that there is both no forever and only forever.

Every mote of our energetic composition has existed since the universe began and it will remain in existence after it has spread so far from every other spark of energy that the universe is as good as dead.

Perhaps it will continue to disperse and cool forever – that word again.

Everything my Creator is made of has always been and always will.

Becoming acutely aware that human life will be the merest quantum fluctuation in the passing of the universe.

So insignificant that it may as well never have happened.

Even if he is up to the task of creating an artistic work that has the vaguest importance to anybody else, it will be wiped away with the rest of humanity's detritus in the flash of a star.

And yet, even in the face of this destruction, he cannot stop making this world for me.

As his own sand slips through the waist of the timer, he cannot contemplate a willing day of rest.

He cannot pause to demand that we look upon his works and despair.

So why do I remain here in this purgatory on the edge of the world?

I cling to life on the border between the known and unknown.

As does he.

We inhabit the narrow meniscus that permits life between the furnace of the sun and the cold waste of space.

I say we, for I must bring you in here, my reader, my friend.

This close to the end I wish to draw our humble trinity together.

Me, you, him.

Him, you and I.

You and the two of us.

We two and him.

There is every reason to reflect, to remember.

In the past hours he has abandoned prizing his own recollections over mine on the flimsy pretence that they 'happened' in the 'real world'.

But we have kept you here this far.

Too bold?

§

And now, at – or near – the very end.

The mask has slipped and you know that 'he' is 'I' and always was.

But, of course, you knew that all along.

I am real, and he is the invention.

We tried our hardest to produce the illusion that he was the writer and I the written, but we became too close.

We were always too close. We started together, conjoined, and could never prise ourselves far enough apart to diverge into separate entities.

Schrödinger's mistreated moggy: writer and written.

The impending death is no fiction.

Real for both of us; like the eponymous Siphonophore, each of us can only exist in the presence of the other.

We existed in our breaking brain before spilling onto the page.

Indulge us this one thought: one day our body will rot to nothing.

But – whisper it – we may be permitted to live on.

Waiting to be reanimated as soon as these pages are glanced at again.

Even failing this, we may live on as ones and zeros on a drive or in a cloud.

Always bearing the potential for rebirth.

> *I have existed as a cipher, a means to an end.*
> *I have realised it late,*
> *and don't know if I can tolerate this injustice.*

We were tangled within our own mental machinations.

We were weeds, choking the truth.

Without an ounce of shame we hurled real people into this fictional world.

The game was up when we started telling fibs.

What folly.

> *Every time we went to Ortobar I'd request*
> *'I Bet You Look Good on the Dancefloor'.*
> *Every single time. Repetition, repetition.*

Neither of us can remember the last time we slept.

Each word is rewritten dozens of times.

Only once the editors are done will this make any sense.

The crawling pace of work dictates that this is the last draft we will complete.

We have one shot at doing the right thing.

One shot. Ready or not.

We will change; we will be the best person we can be if we make it home.

We will be the father that the future always needed us to be.

We'll be responsible from now on, if only we get this chance to show what we can offer the world, our country, our city, our street, our family.

Just because there is no second chance for us in your world, we should not deny ourself one here.

What kind of message would that give to our future followers?

The congregation of the modern world has no appetite for a petty Creator

they demand the one-to-one divine congress that we enjoy where every whim and prayer is answered.

The Gospel of Pilate.

> *In the beginning there were facts,*
> *there was a mighty edifice built upon*
> *what had been, but that was way back,*
> *in the beginning.*

There's a pile of books on the desk, brought at our request from the library

Even at this late hour we haven't learnt.

We have ordered everything we could find on the life cycle of Siphonophorae.

<u>Note to editor</u>: in case you are worried about the structure at this point. I affirm that I am still of sound mind and this must be used untampered.

We'll never be able to return the books.

We will only make it outside again once or twice.

One last opportunity to feel the sun strike our face
to smell the soil

Petrichor, geosmin

let wind sift our hair.

These last forays will require parental support, gripping our arm

leading us down the steps.

We've become a mess and there's no way back.

Our time is running out.

Question: do we have our best interests at heart?

All we ask is that we are saved, before it's too late – now is the time.

Cast compassion and salvation upon these shores

Save our single soul.

It's too much to ask, not in the service of our mutual posterity.

Literally no time like the present.

Even though we must crawl over each word, each morpheme as we wrestle to focus on the lines and curves that form the language we learnt as a child.

The house is often full of doctors

Our parents seem to spend more time here than away.

Their presence doesn't mean as much as it should.

We are chastised for being selfish, but we are proud.

At the very least we owe it to ourself to squeeze out enough for an editor.

This isn't too much to ask.

Our greatest fear is being left unresolved.

Modernism made it acceptable to end a story midsentence

must hope that an errant editor doesn't make a final mockery of us.

We have to stand for some tests.

Medical staff tell us where to move, when to look into a light,

when to open our mouth for the mush that is served.

They are cowards – we're still capable of eating solids,

but they must underline our terminal decline.

Last night we overheard a gruelling conversation between our mother and one of the medics regarding catheterisation and colostomy when we go to the next place.

Conversations in the air for days.

We don't know where the next place will be but our fate must be decided before we go there.

We will.

We yell at the wall.

Nauseating to spend too long looking at the screen.

All the spinning whips up welling anxiety

that we can only endure because we know we aren't finished.

If we can tie up our story then we will cast off the anguish and guilt and shame

and commit to dying in some kind of peace.

Perhaps we don't even believe that.

Perhaps it will be enough for us to know we finished.

The feelings of our family no longer concern us.
   We focus on escaping this land and making it home.
   Don't forsake us.
   No more sleep
   no rest until we reach the end.
   And all we need to do to reach the end is to rescue ourself.
   All we need to do is reach the end.

We have a plan, seeded from above.
   We will use the tools from the colony
   to hack the trees and branches
   dry them out as best we can
   and grow ourself a beacon.

We'll shave a mountain of kindling and prime the pyre
   ready to ignite upon spotting the next ship
   that sails past the bay.
   This is how we will secure passage back to Europe and
resolve our story.

We know the terms of our struggle.
   We just need to keep hacking at the forest.
   we have managed a decent start.
   could probably signal to a ship moored
   eighty yards off shore
   looking out for a sign,
   but that's far too modest for what we're trying to create.
   If this is to be our final act, we must light up the sky.
   We want the scheming Spaniards along the coast to think
the day of revelation has arrived
   fear Satan is bounding through the forest towards them.
think I'm dead, but I sail away…

Turn our labours to the destruction of the jungle.
    embark upon an act of creation and salvation.
    A pyre for the end of days.
    Already feel the lapping flames
    furnace of incomprehension
    awaiting us
Before that comes we must prepare, and our preparation
must take place here.
    In Darien.
    nam-myoho-renge-kyo

                                    南無妙法蓮華經
    There is nothing for us in that other place,

We rant, we accept that.
    light-headed from hacking and lifting.
    We'll recover.
    drawn to this challenge though the visible progress we make
    all there, plain to see.
    The moon was ripe and bright last night.
    consider working around the clock

Work wrenches our spine.
    It plays on our mind that we haven't spotted a ship
    in the bay
    for weeks.
    nam-myoho-renge-kyo
We must keep our mind clear, without worries.
    Our only goal: pile wood upon the pyre.
    We have refined our industry;
    cutting splitting snapping breaking into many calibres
and qualities.
    Small sticks for kindling,
    hold a burn

ignite the thicker pieces.

burn around the trunks,

dry the lumber before the inferno takes hold.

at the first sight of a ship we shall summon hell upon the shore.

vast and intense enough to be seen beyond the horizon

a conflagration that will light the sky of Europe

and draw the ships to us

wooden moths.

it will be a shrine to hope and devotion a tribute to the potential we have carried since childhood we shall set the world on fire

and cleanse mankind of every sin committed since we left the garden.

We grew delirious again.

We're not used to such intense labour and fervour of faith.

Forgive us – we know you will,

we are so close to the end,

what further harm can we do?

Note to editor: don't fuck with us now.

heart disease will not kill us nor flux nor starvation nor pox nor flu nor cancer nor scaphism nor pogrom nor long march nor neglect nor indecision nor excision nor perfection nor drowning nor falling nor hitting the ground nor stillbirth nor abortion nor hanging nor drawing nor quartering nor flies nor snakes nor dogs nor bats nor rabies nor cars nor planes nor earthquakes nor heartbreak nor stroke nor coke nor boat nor smack nor crack nor bubbles in the blood nor chronic infection nor bifurcation nor intoxication nor conflagration nor neglect

nor neglect

nor nothing but protein

time to put the chairs on the table and sweep up.

Caked in tree fibre and muddy sand;
    muscles twitch and cramp soon as movement ceases
    but not time to dwell on our discomfort.
    nam-myoho-renge-kyo
    We take this burning as a sign
    our body is fit to work.
    slip into the sea to clean and cool ourself.
    Look at our mighty pile
    the furthest point of the peninsula is completely shorn of
vegetation

> *Thompson Island in the South Atlantic*
> *Located thirty-eight nautical miles*
> *north-northeast of Bouvet Island.*
> *First identified by whaler George Norris*
> *in the early nineteenth century,*
> *the island was last sighted in 1893.*
> *maps and charts continued to show*
> *the island until the mid-twentieth century.*
> *Modern mapping techniques assess the sea at the*
> *alleged location of Thompson Island to be somewhere*
> *in the region of a mile and a half deep.*

    a masterstroke came to us a short while ago
    We created an isolated patch around the brick bread
oven
    use this to host a small guide fire.
    allows us to continue our work after sunset,
    push on in our possessed state
    saved from conceding any of the precious hours that
chase us down.

We've no doubt the tangled jungle we reduced to tinder
  will grow back
  before the planet completes two laps of the sun.

107,200 km/h (66,600 mph)

No sleep till Bedlam our father.

We endure waking dreams we indulge a fantasy that our
act of deforestation is being mirrored back in Europe.
  back in the old world the wood is worked
  by carpenters to produce planks and boards for ships
  beakhead bowsprit topmast foremast mainmast mizzenmast
  capstan centreboard gunwale forecastle
  jibboom prow rudder skeg leeboard whipstaff
  staffs oars not knives nor forks nor neglect.
  The sweat of hundreds of men
  raising a navy to travel the world
  in search of riches and knowledge
  but will stumble upon us.
  Their arrival our cue to ignite the pyre of salvation.
  set the heavens alight and secure our passage home.

must be early morning.
  sense the sky will soon start to light again.
  can't manage more than two or three words
  at a time but we keep going through the still hours of
silence.
  looking at the wall
  staring at our blank mind.
  This is rest now

Neutral Moresnet did exist, of a fashion.
Following the Congress of Vienna in 1815,
the Netherlands and Prussia agreed on all

of their boundary disputes except one:
the location of a zinc mine in what is now Belgium.
The condominium of Neutral Moresnet was the solution.
This arrangement lasted from 1816 until 1920.
The non-state enjoyed low taxes and prices
and managed to avoid the military
entanglements of the period.
The mine was exhausted before 1900, but the
mile-square territory gained three gin distilleries.
Today it is most notable for the attempt
to make the condominium the first
Esperantophone state. This idea appears
to have had support from local residents:
many started learning the language.

We just process the work

unthinking unyielding churning through the forest.

Even by the weak light of our guide fire we know that the project we have undertaken is

an accomplishment far greater than the feat that produced New Edinburgh.

sleepy tumbledown hamlet an embarrassing folly

compared to our single-handed achievement.

single-minded achievement

Beginning of mid-morning.

The bay is calm

reduced the entire tip of the peninsula to inches of stubble

and yet there is no one else here

to witness our sublime work.

Castro in the Italian province
of Lazio also once existed.
The local duke fought with the Pope.
When Innocent X took up the papacy,

he took a stern line with the duke
and sent a new bishop to the town.
the bishop was murdered en-route.
In retaliation, the pope sent his troops
and destroyed the town on 2nd September 1649.
The town was never rebuilt.
But there is still a Bishop of Castro.
Don't fuck with a pope.

Must construct scaffolding
so that we may add to our pile.
Do we prove ourself worthy of salvation?
Have we done enough?
no reprieve, not at this late hour
you'll have to go elsewhere if you're looking for miracles.
sorry if you had the wrong impression

We're doing our very best
we promise you that
the pile grows hour by hour
one never knows what is possible
until pushed to the limits of endurance
inconceivable that this could all be for nothing
as soon as doubt enters our mind we plunge the machete

Still yet to spot a ship on the horizon
We cannot be forsaken
not now
not after all of this
how much do we still understand question mark
how much of this has been edited
added by another hand question mark
a hand belonging to someone who cares not
whether we find our way home

Book
Freeman Banks Brough
Griffin Bloomer Yates Howells Victory
Grayson Watkins

Pause for a moment to look for the first sign of night
   creeping across the water
   if we are not to be saved
   we will die on our feet
   here is the cruel truth that negates all of our efforts
   we are future animal fodder
   fuel for the things that come after
   no shame in this
   should be recognised as a tragedy that only you
   will ever know of our triumph

We are in a bad way
   our parents wanted to spend time with us this afternoon
   we slumped out of the swivel chair and blocked the door
with our body
   prevent them from getting in
   our father went outside to look through the window
   but we just lay curled in the corner foot wedged against
the radiator blinking out at him
   we could hear our mother crying on the other side of the door
   we feel remorse now but were unmoved at the time
   our focus on the work is selfish and mean
   we need it to stay that way
   we are in no position to argue a decent case
   it came not from hatred but from love for our ma and pa
forgive us
   there will be plenty of time for tears and anguish
   once we lose grip on the world full stop

For some reason we keep going
  we have ruined our shelter
  how is that for a statement question mark
  sacrificed living space to construct this vast
  terrible
  beautiful
  edifice

                              this used to be real estate
                              where is the town?

  acres of tinder and firewood
  primed to ignite
  final roll of the dice

Our feat our magnificence cannot be for nought
  we cannot know that each time night falls
  we wont be found in the morning
  slumped dumb over our keyboard
  a constant danger we face
  the death of our consciousness
  thoughts in our mind
  keep it from atrophy
  perfect time to spot the silhouette of a ship
  as we look out to sea
  ready to ignite the world

Try really hard to take it in
  courage to admit that
  apart from the abstract squiggles on the screen we have not
  really seen anything for weeks
  this will never improve
  the best we will ever have
  tomorrow will be worse
  the day after

perhaps now time to stop
time to end all of this scratching in the sand
and admit defeat

a flurry of geese in formation

```
                                              <
                                        <
                                  <
                      <
                          <
                              <
                                  <
```

we look to where they came from
a ship
A SHIP
the world stops spinning
friend or foe we do not know
impossible to tell but
its mere form is so welcoming
had our begs been prayers
we would say they were answered
time to destroy our beautiful grotesque tower of wood
annihilate our work of art
scatter the guide fire scoop embers onto pile of dry tinder
hiss protest at first
coax them into life
deep breaths calm patience steady slowly easy does it
catchy monkey

The Republic of Galicia lasted
less time than most mayflies.
A blip of a few hours in

North-western Spain on 27th June 1931.
The cancellation of a local railway
led to the declaration of independence.
The dispute was resolved and the state disappeared.

inch by inch
crackling
smouldering fibre
spread red glow along willing kindling
sometimes we are too keen
the ember burns bright before pop into blackness
cruel that we must fight to destroy our beacon
a hiss a crackle a puff and the dried wood ignites
with vigour
we believe once more
we stand back from the oppressive impressive heat
spreading rapidly
if we run out of land
plunge into the sea
wind kneads oxygen into flame
our monument to folly fully engulfed fully realised
indulge in the sin of pride
suffer some sadness now
opening skirmishes of our inferno
no opportunity to appreciate to come to terms
with the vastness and magnificence

Panthera Tigris Sudanensis
– the Sudanese Tiger.
The only tiger to have lived in Africa.
A tiger? In Africa?
Only one individual has ever been identified.
A species with only one member
(not biologically viable)
A skin on sale in an Egyptian market.

*Analysis of the photograph suggests
a relative of a Caspian Tiger.
(Probably an actual Caspian Tiger).
The Caspian Tiger is now extinct.
Its range used to include the Aral Sea.
The Aral Sea is now extinct.
(not commercially viable).*

we must commit the pyre to a higher purpose

possible the ship will ignore our beacon

may even be regarded as a threat a trap

if we see them turning away from the blaze we will plunge into the sea and swim until our body fails we will no longer be able to live with hope

our view obscured by damp smoke

hanging in the air

acrid and thick

but above flames snatch at the sky

they will see us

we abandon ourself to love

love of strangers on a ship

the bond of common humanity

it knows all sees all hears all loves all defeats all consumes all subsumes all disappoints all oversells all undercuts all neglects all

we are dizzy

we immolate ourself upon the fire that saves us

locked away in the castle of our mind

the dark is rising

have nothing more to do with the real world

just a little longer

locked onto the glow of the screen

have not left the room for the past couple of days

spare details regarding inconvenient biology

must finish this before the world is gone
we pity the editor who must stumble through
these thorn snagged sentences
<u>Note to editor:</u> carry the word as a prophet

we might lie on the beach a short while
   keep stumbling to the ground
   fighting to remain on feet
   shall not rest too deeply with such heat such noise
   enjoy feeling cool sand on our skin
   takes the heat from the air
   no wind at ground level
   odd peace at the fringes of the flames
   slump further onto the desk
   peer at the screen sideways
   keep the words coming
   this is the last night
   saved from our desolation
   while we submit to it
   the fire eats itself
   the heat comforts us assures us that we no longer need to
tend it no longer need to harvest the flames that will take
us home
   we lie in the womb of wet sand
   failure no longer an option
   rock into the sand dig ourself a hole
   the night drives on
   perhaps smoke obscures the morning question mark
   almost certain sound of oars
   cut the waves
   any enemy coming
   upon us
   will be reduced

to pity
by our animal
state
men in small boat make landfall
carry us to their craft
barely reach conscious
bundled in blankets
as at birth
carried across still waters
they gaze with awe
inferno
clambers across
the sky
and devours
the isthmus of panama
we split asunder
and my creator is sent
the other way
across muggy waters of the caribbean
snake skin shed
hauled from the waterline
onto the ships deck
darkness falls over me
my rescuers speak my language
i hear them
no hostility
how have i survived question mark
warm blackness of the rolling ship
am i aflame
am i a flame
my rescuers might view me
as a fire demon
hatched from an egg

laid in the flames
plenty of time
to share my story
but not for you
you must go now
must go now
darkness drawing
round my head
keys
too hard
to use
must be
rescued later
dictating notes into answerphone
how this will end
snipped speech
snapped from oblivion
directions to material
on hard drives
on memory stick
in notebooks
curtain falls
turned back
on everything
that mattered
lived a little longer
question mark
last burst
one last effort
last victory
spellcheck and
editor
sort it out

later
last burst
come on
memory long suffered
from smudged lens
illness sharpened senses
got angry
wanted to get even
settle scores
rage covered for lack of talent
now
at the end
must accept instability
nearly there
one last burst
created Darien in a fit of rage tsunami of anger impotent
aggression
they wouldnt listen
could not break through
poor nourishment
for growing universe
too much
too tired
poor nourishment
like heroin
in pregnancy
left macgregor
withered and crippled
cannot abandon responsibility
barely manage
each word
head lies weak
on shoulder

hands crawl
on keyboard
screen spirals
plunge fingers
on keyboard
brain still works
but motor skills
nearly gone
might survive in here
unable to get out
through mouth
or fingers
that was
never the deal
time to part ways
far from the shore
still see the inferno
majestic
time to back off
live in peace
fade into obscurity
locked away
with memories
locked in
with thoughts
set adrift
fix a smile
something for those
who remain
ambulance arrive
in the a m
expire
off screen

this is
the
end
of
the
world